With her legs raised on a footrest nearby, her dress had slipped up several inches, leaving her lower thighs exposed. As she awoke she noticed her bare legs in front of her and casually reached down to smooth out her skirt. When she did so, she heard a man's voice coming from the door.

"I was rather hoping you wouldn't do that..."

Lacy froze. Then she finished smoothing her skirt, tucked her legs under her as gracefully as she could and stood up. Turning to face the man to whom the voice belonged, she saw he was smiling roguishly and felt her face redden. She tried not to smile back, but did not succeed. His face had a boylike charm. They both chuckled and he spoke again, his voice calm and soft, which only made her strain to listen harder.

"I'm sorry if I startled you, but you looked so cozy, I didn't want to wake you. My name is Francis Doyle, but I would like it very much if you called me Frank."

. . .

Unlikely Paradise

By: J. M. Maxim

My Dearest Robertson Family, May your smile never fade and your heart be filled with Love Always,

James Maxim

ISBN-13: 978-1475138306
ISBN-10: 147513830X

This is a work of fiction.
Any resemblance to actual persons,
places or events is purely coincidental.

Dedication:

To my family, friends and anyone who is willing to battle mediocrity, despair and darkness, in order to lead a life full of joy, romance and love.

"Take away love and our earth is a tomb."
- Robert Browning

Table of Contents

Chapter 1: The Assignment

Not usually one to wimp out, Lacy felt ashamed for what she was about to do. She stood quietly in the editor's cluttered office, summoning courage. Glancing around at the signed photos of celebrities, designers and writers didn't help, so she instead turned to the wall of glass on her right. The office was on the 38th floor and looked out over bustling Manhattan. It was a view she never grew tired of, regardless of the weather. She took a deep breath, straightening her spine. She felt strong, she felt confident. She looked Barbara Livingston right in the eye. And quietly began to whine.

"But Barbara, I don't think I'm up to this." *You know this won't help*, she told herself.

"Lacy, darling, I love you. You know I love you like a daughter. I've watched you grow in this business and followed your career closer than my own. But I didn't get to be chief editor of this magazine by sending the wrong people to get the job done. Now, I know you and what's-his-face didn't work out..."

"Robert. His *name* is Robert." She felt a bit upset that Barbara had forgotten him already; it had only been a week.

"No Lacy darling, his name *was* Robert and he was a jerk. And you've been working so hard, it's a good time for you to get away. This is just what you need. You'll thank me later, Godivas and flowers will be fine." Barbara smiled a small smile and winked.

"But I'll miss Josephine's birthday party if I go!" It was a long shot, but there was a note of truth in this. Barbara's daughter had been a constant source of joy to both of them since the moment of her birth.

She reached down into the chaotic collection of papers, photos, typeset mockups and layout designs that Barbara somehow operated so efficiently behind, picking up a framed picture of the three of them. Lacy's rich, auburn hair had grown since the photograph and was now a few inches past her shoulders, spiraling into the long, wispy curls that she had such difficulty taming. She fondly remembered the warm spring day, earlier this year, when they took that picture at the Brooklyn Zoo. She had a copy on her desk as well. At the time, she was between disastrous relationships and was taking advantage of having some free time.

In the photograph, she was wearing her favorite jeans (the ones that fit her slim figure perfectly) and what Barbara always called "the most important accessory," a bright, wide smile. At five feet, six inches tall, she knew she fell within the average range, but Barbara had been a model in her youth, rising several inches above six feet in flat-soled shoes. In the picture she seemed to tower over Lacy. The adorable, eight *"but I'm almost nine"* year-old, Josephine, stood between them, clutching a stuffed parrot and a cone of cotton candy. Her small, proud smile beamed between pink-stained cheeks. Lacy put the frame back on Barbara's desk. She often told her friends that Barbara Livingston was not only her friend and mentor but also the most elegant woman she'd ever met.

Now Barbara smiled wider than before and, curling her short hair behind her ears, stood up, walked around her desk and grasped Lacy's shoulders. "Darling," she said, "I need this. You need this too. Not just to get away, but because it's the cover story and a great opportunity for you. Also, I need my best on it. You're my best and you know it. We'll save you some cake and you can take us for tea in a few weeks."

Lacy grinned sheepishly. Truth to be told, there was nothing she wouldn't do for Barbara. She had never had a closer, more compassionate friend. "Yeah, I know...but who's going to cover the Flower Show..."

"Please!" Barbara said through peals of laughter, releasing Lacy's shoulders to turn towards the desk. "I'll find *somebody* to cover the annual convention of Bulb Beaters! You just get the story on this Francis Doyle. You'll find everything you need in here." She handed her a large folder. "Your train leaves at four and don't forget your camera." At this Lacy brightened slightly; she loved traveling by train. But looking up at Barbara's face raised eyebrow she heard, "But lest you feel spoiled, you're *not* renting a convertible when you get there! We're a good magazine, but we're not that good! Not until you write your amazing cover story, that is."

They both laughed this time and after saying goodbyes, Lacy walked out. She would not disappoint Barbara if she could help it. But a week in New Hampshire wasn't her idea of a dream vacation. She'd been a city girl for five years now and she saw no reason to change. True, it was a difficult adjustment at first. The bright lights and noisy traffic had led to some sleepless nights. The oppressiveness of gigantic buildings, constant movement and hordes of people sometimes made her ache for quiet strolls through long blades of grass; someplace she could allow the constant state of alertness to drop. But soon enough the conveniences and sparkling social opportunities won her over. By now she knew she could survive on her own and that meant everything.

She stepped out of the tower of glass and steel and looked up to see that it was a bright, sunny afternoon. *At least the weather looks good,* she thought as she hailed a cab. Sighing, she gave the cabbie instructions to her apartment and leaned back in the torn seat. Feeling a curved shard of aged vinyl dig into her shoulder, she thought better of it and sat up straight as best as she could. She focused on trying to ignore how much she loved New York this time of year; late summer, cooling into fall. *It's only one week. I can handle a week. I'll be back here, stuck in traffic, soon enough.*

She packed quickly, taking mostly basic items; favorite running sneakers, a couple of pairs of pajama bottoms, a large-brimmed straw hat, sunglasses and a gentle perfume. *This was going to be done in comfort*, she thought. She heard her cell phone buzzing in her purse and fished it out. *Barbara again*, she thought, rolling her eyes. *She really is worse than a mother sometimes.*

"Darling, don't forget to bring something nice, in case you have to go out to dinner." She didn't hide the mischief in her voice very well.

"Barbara, for goodness sake, I'm going to write a cover story, not get a date!"

"Lacy Stockton! Francis Doyle has money and not a lot of spare time. He also hasn't had any noteworthy female companionship in a while. And *no,* you may not ask how I know that. He may want to have a dinner meeting someplace nice and I don't want you to go walking in wearing jeans and a tee, got it? Remember you represent the magazine..."

"Barbara, I'm not having some rich guy take me out. I'll expense the whole thing, you got that?"

"Whatever it takes, darling, whatever it takes!" As Barbara started to laugh heartedly, Lacy hung up on her. Then she laughed herself. *That woman needs a sexual lobotomy! Still...*She thought about it and decided to pack the sexy, low-cut, black dress she got last week at Neiman Marcus and some high, glossy, patent leather, open-toed stilettos. Glancing briefly at the bright red soles of the shoes, she thought that if it was necessary, at least she could make sure she had the upper hand. She grabbed some cute underwear and some *cuter* underwear. Ramming them into her leather traveling bag, she shook her head, disgruntled that Barbara had this kind of power over her. Then she pulled on fresh jeans, her boots and a light, snug sweater and headed off to Grand Central.

Chapter 2: The Case File

It was turning out to be a lovely ride. Lacy had always loved trains. Her grandfather was an engineer working the Amtrak Northeast Corridor lines and she had practically grown up at the station near her childhood home in Mystic, Connecticut. The rhythmic click-clack and occasional side-to-side sway was comforting. The train was like a large, capable dance partner and she felt secure once it had taken the lead. She sat back, watching the countryside flow by, letting the New York tension she had learned to live with melt, inch by inch, from her shoulders and neck. Sipping at a thick white paper cup of hot chocolate, she slouched into the seat and stretched her legs in front of her.

"Hmmm..." she hummed, opening the file from Barbara. Her eyebrows arched when she saw a picture of a tall, handsome man wearing a dark suit staring back at her. It was a clipping from the *West Dobley Courier,* a small New Hampshire newspaper. The caption read, *"Francis and Martha Doyle announce the opening of Haven, a new, luxury bed & breakfast in West Dobley, NH."* There was a woman standing next to him, older, shorter and elegantly dressed in pearls and a dark, simply cut gown. She shared the same fierce eyes. *Clearly his mother.* The date of the clipping was almost five years ago and it wasn't the best shot, but not so fuzzy that Lacy couldn't see the well-developed figure Mr. Doyle possessed, enhanced by the impeccably cut suit.

None of that, she warned herself. The last month with *what's-his-face* had been so annoying that she planned on giving up on men entirely for a while. Before Robert it had been a string of nightmare dates; dates that usually ended with her standing up and leaving and *never* ended with her even remotely interested in a second meeting. Barbara said the only reason she had settled for the emotionally detached, unmotivated Robert, albeit briefly, was due to a phenomenon she called "learned helplessness." She could still hear her wise friend's words in her head, "If someone is tortured long enough, Lacy darling, they give up on any possibility of controlling their own destiny. You've had so many bad dates that you ran to the shelter of his selfish, needy behavior just to feel *wanted!*" It was a tough lesson, but she had learned it. *It's true what they say,* she thought, *people treat you exactly how you allow them to treat you.*

She wasn't really even that upset over Robert, somehow she had known she deserved better from the start. It wasn't that. It was more about the weary, tiresome game of disappointment; the hope, the reckoning and the defeat, seemingly cycled ad infinitum.

Her clock hadn't quite started to strike, thankfully. She wasn't eager to marry. She wasn't ready for children, at least not yet. But the city, for all of its excitement and magic, could sometimes be a lonely place. She enjoyed time to herself and knew the value of quiet, reflective moments. Still, nights when the rain muffles the sounds of traffic and a glass of good red wine makes her feel cozy, frisky and talkative, she longed for someone to know her; someone she actually wanted to know, as well.

Shaking her head to clear it, she reminded herself to focus on the job. *Looks like Barbara did her homework on this one,* she thought, lifting one eyebrow as she paged through the heavy file. There were more clippings, celebrity sightings, charity balls and other press releases about many of the hot spots in the town. A few minutes later, feeling more aware of what she was getting herself into, she closed the file and stared out the window. She had passed the edges of the city some time ago and now saw only small towns; small towns, fields and lots of cows.

I've got to pull it together, she told herself firmly. *This is the cover story; Romantic Bed & Breakfasts of New England – Haven, Winner of House to Home's most exclusive award!* She tried to take some notes from the extensive file, but kept glancing back to the picture in the front. *Hmmm...looks like six-two...maybe six-three? Dark hair... Twenty-eight? Thirty-three? Why can't men age like women?* His eyes definitely had a tale to tell, seeming to gleam through the black and white clipping. He did not look at all like how she thought the owner of a New Hampshire B&B would look. *Lacy Stockton! Show some backbone!* She closed the file and stuffed it in her bag, frustrated with her lack of discipline. Maybe getting away was what she needed. Maybe this trip wouldn't be quite so painful. *Maybe I need a lobotomy, too.* She chuckled softly to herself and settled into the train's rocky sway for the remainder of the trip.

Chapter 3: Hot Wheels

When she arrived that evening she stepped off the train feeling relaxed, clear headed and ready for business. The train had stopped at West Dobley station, but the chirping of crickets and jagged outline of tall pines made it clear that they were several miles from the center of town. It seemed strange at first, since she was used to hopping on the subway and hopping off within blocks, *sometimes within feet*, of where she wanted to go. *At least the car agency is close,* she thought. Collecting her things, she asked the porter where she could find the rental counter. When he pointed her across the terminal, she started off, a look of mischief creeping over her face as she thought of renting a convertible just to get even with Barbara. At any rate, it would be nice to be behind the wheel in a car. She hadn't driven in quite some time; the city didn't need any more traffic and parking was a nightmare anyway. *Doubt I'll have that problem here*, she thought with a small laugh.

After waiting in line for a minute, while a slightly-too-cutesy couple, dressed in matching black and white plaid shirts and tan Dockers, decided whether or not they needed to upgrade, she got to the counter. The woman waiting behind the counter looked friendly, almost fanatically so, and with a warm smile she asked, "May I help you dear?"

"Lacy Stockton, I have a reservation." She found herself smiling back in response. *Must be something in the air...besides manure and cut grass.*

"Lacy Stockton...Laceeeeyy Stocktonnnn..." The woman's name tag read Beverly and her shoulder-length, blonde hair jumped and dived as the woman nodded her head rapidly, like a dashboard bobblehead. "Oh yes! I remember. We got a call about you from a Barbara Livingston; she made sure we were to give you a convertible. Lacy's eyes brightened and her smile widened. *Good ol' Barbara.* "Let's see...here it is...Ford Mustang convertible, space 12 out front. You have a good time, sweetheart."

"Thank you," Lacy replied and met the woman's broad grin with one of her own. Walking out the front doors of the station, she saw the rental lot not too far off and to the right. She felt a flutter of fear, realizing the parking lot was quite dark. Then she realized it was almost empty as well. *Relax Lacy, you're not in New York anymore, remember?*

"That's right," she spoke out loud and quickly looked around to verify that no one had heard her, or was looking at her like she was crazy. Taking a deep breath, she caught the strong scent of pine, fresh cut grass and moisture. Her skin tingled with the sensations caused by a damp, cool breeze easing by. She walked to the car, her favorite color, metallic red, and got in. Locking the doors, she turned the key and put on the high beams. She couldn't help thinking it was nice to be able to use high beams at night without blinding half a dozen drivers every other minute, not to mention having to deal with horns, yells, etc. *Ok, so it has its charms. Now where's that address? Can't do a cover story on the prettiest cow field in New Hampshire, can I?*

She grabbed the pink, square note Barbara had clipped to the front of the file and observed, for the first time, the name of the road the inn was on; One Strawberry Lane. *I'll bet that works on the tourists, Mr. Doyle.* The GPS in the dashboard dinged cheerfully, the display stating that West Dobley center was within fifteen minutes of the station. She pulled out of the lot and after a few curves on a dark, tree-lined Route-something-or-other, the exit was in sight.

Turning onto Main Street, she casually glanced out the window to find chocolate shops, antique stores, the Chamber of Commerce, gourmet coffee shops, boutique clothiers and even a place where you could rent a horse and buggy for a thirty minute trip around the large central commons. Despite the reaction she planned to have when she saw the town, she had to admit it was actually one of the most adorable, charming and romantic places she had ever seen. Everything had a sleepy, dreamlike, vaguely European quality and she was pleasantly surprised to find herself falling victim to its charms. Even from a casual drive, she could see that details had mattered; from the windows and signage, to the sidewalks and street lamps. It was as if someone had opened an old, treasured book of fairy tales and she had driven her rented convertible right into the pages.

The commons was empty and apparently all the shops closed at 7 p.m. during the week, except for a few sleepy taverns and restaurants. Not a soul was on the brightly lit street and few cars were parked, but she could sense the sudden emptiness that only comes from places that are usually quite populous and are caught at a rare moment of peace.

"This guy has a goldmine here," she murmured as she passed a very cozy looking *Hibernatin' Bear* bookstore.

At the edge of several acres of green space that made up the commons, she turned left onto Strawberry Lane. Passing an ornate, wrought iron gate, she followed the slight curves of the road until she began to realize something. *This is not a road...it's a driveway!* Sure enough, she had driven about half a mile, when coming around a bend she saw the winner of her beloved House To Home magazine's most prestigious award looming before her.

Chapter 4: Haven

Haven reminded her more of a blue-blood estate than a bed and breakfast. Two stories high, gleaming white and enormous, it stood proud and perfect. Built in the early 1900s, she remembered reading something from the file that mentioned the architect basing his designs on a palace in Europe. It was originally built as a summer home for a very wealthy industrialist and no expense had been spared. The driveway ran straight from where it left the tree line, alongside an emerald lawn big enough to have a football game on. Then it turned to the right, widened and looped around a magnificent fountain, before continuing on through an arch to what she assumed was a garage area.

The fountain was twenty feet tall at its highest point and depicted Triton astride a sea horse, battling a creature of the deep. Riding his mount into the sky atop a mighty breaker, the large figure and entire scene was showered with tubes of water that shot from points within the great battle, cascading down to the collecting pool. As Lacy drove towards it, she could swear she saw the muscular forms flex and slowly bend with the eternal struggle.

Haven was built on a slight rise, allowing occupants to gaze over the fountain and driveway from its many windows. It stood, peacefully beckoning viewers to come and see the spectacle.

Lacy couldn't remember seeing a more hospitable location.

Directly behind the fountain was an overhanging roof that created a carriage depot. The columns were thick and white, and Lacy doubted she could fit her arms around them. The whole area grew thick with Moonflower and Morning Glory, the flowering vines obviously chosen with care to ensure deep blue blossoms were open all day, while the pale, white batch took over and opened at night. The thick blossoms were changing shift as she drove up, filling the air with a sweet scent. The roof of the carriage port was a balcony, with French doors leading into the second story.

A porter met her at the steps. He wore a crisp uniform, brass buttons shining in rows on his wine-colored jacket. Sharp creases on his black pants met his polished shoes with an exactness that appeared almost military.

"Good evening, ma'am. If you'll be good enough to give me the keys, I'll park your car in the garage and bring the bags up to your room." He wasn't more then twenty years old, but his voice, kind and serious, lent him an air of maturity. Lacy handed him the keys to the rental and began to fumble in her purse for a tip.

"That won't be necessary, Miss Stockton." The porter smiled and walked towards the car. Lacy stood for a second, mouth open, before smiling and walking towards the inn. *I've never met a porter that wouldn't love a tip. Either Francis Doyle pays very well, or he's a slave driver.*

The two doors were almost nine feet in height, very dark wood, with brass trim and heavy knockers. They had small, oval windows of cut glass at roughly eye height, ornate but not overdone in any way. Just as Lacy was thinking about how she was going to get one of the behemoths to open for her, it swung inwards suddenly and a man burst out, almost running her over.

"Oh! Excuse me!" Lacy shrieked, jumping aside.

The man glanced at her briefly. Scowling and catching only a glimpse of her, he hurried down the steps and to the left, towards the small drive that led to the garage.

"Well!" Lacy said to his back. "I'm fine, thank you!" As the man made no sign of slowing or apologizing, she picked up her purse where she had dropped it. Glancing back over her shoulder, she started up the three stairs to the door, which was slow to close. She was on the second step when she stopped, glancing back at the figure hustling off. *Was that him? Could that careless wall of flesh have been Francis Doyle?* She thought about it for a moment. He seemed to have the same intense eyes, but it had happened too fast for her to positively identify him. She shrugged her shoulders and walked through the door, only to stop dead again after stepping a few feet into the lobby.

She stood transfixed by the beautiful space, until hearing the door click quietly shut behind her. The floors were white marble. Twenty feet ahead and to the right stood the check-in counter, fashioned of the same dark wood as the door and accented by the same brass furnishings.

Directly ahead of her was a sitting area, composed of a luxurious couch and two overstuffed chairs nestled on a large Persian rug. Beyond the furniture was an enormous fireplace, eight feet wide and tall enough for her to stand inside and brush her hair without soiling her blouse. Between the fireplace and the counter was a wide staircase, composed of the same white marble as the floor, with wrought iron railings.

Everything was polished to a mirror shine and Lacy momentarily felt self-conscious. *Glad I wore jeans! If it wasn't for these strategically placed Persians, anything above the knee would let this beautiful lobby see too much of its guests!*

"Good evening, Miss Stockton." Until then, Lacy hadn't realized there was anybody else in the lobby. Now she saw a kindly looking gentleman coming out of a small office behind the counter. He was smiling and immediately reminded Lacy of her grandfather. Dressed in a similar style as the porter, he carried himself with the same intelligent, hospitable posture. Suddenly she realized the porter had known her name as well. "My name is Howard. I have your room ready, as well as a message for you, if you would like to take it now."

UNLIKELY PARADISE

"Hello Howard. I would love to see my room and take my message, if you would help me understand something."

"Of course, Miss Stockton, anything I can do"

"Well," she smiled, "you can start by calling me Lacy and you can continue by telling me how everyone here knows my name?"

He smiled, sort of embarrassed, but not at all patronizing. "We don't get many walk-ins, Miss Stockton...I mean Miss Lacy. The entire crew is briefed on the guests twenty-four hours before they are scheduled to arrive. We are given photographs if available, if not we just do the best we can based on physical descriptions and an E.T.A."

"I see," she said, but actually didn't see at all. In fact she had never seen anything like it before.

"Yes, it's all part of welcoming you home." He smiled broadly after saying this. "By the way, the chef is on duty twenty-four-seven, if you feel at all hungry. Our restaurant, Sanctuary, is highly rated by Zagat and has been awarded three Michelin stars. New French-wave, cultural pocket Italian, with local ingredients thrown in for good measure, but don't let them scare you. Some amazing meals, to be sure, but they also make a great meatloaf sandwich and their mac-and-cheese is to die for.

We have a masseuse, art teacher, personal trainer and tennis, horseback, firearms and yoga coaches. They make regular appearances at least once a week. The pool, gym, spa and indoor golf facilities are one flight down. There's a small salon downstairs too; great straight razor shaves, but I hear the color treatments and other services are excellent too. In fact, Diane, the house stylist has been recruited by so many celebrities that she has an agent of her own!"

"Wow!" laughed Lacy. "Thanks for the rundown, Howard. I'm sure I'll be very happy here."

When Howard spoke, pride in his job and this facility was obvious. He beamed with it. He was incredibly attentive and eager to please. "Yes, Miss Lacy. I think you will. If there is anything you need, just dial zero and I'll be there in a flash. Room number eight, up the stairs and to the right. I'll make sure Jonathan has collected your baggage and we'll meet you up there in just a few minutes."

"Oh! Howard, who was that man?"

"Ma'am?"

"Some angry looking man just tried to show me the way out, while I was on my way in. You didn't see him?"

"Sorry, Miss Lacy, I was in the office. It's soundproofed to keep the fax machine, copier and phone from disturbing the guests. Would you like me to have the grounds checked?"

"Oh no, that's not necessary, just wanted to know if you knew him."

"Well, the grounds are checked every hour anyway, we take our guests' privacy very seriously. I'll just call and have them checked just in case."

"If you really think you should, it was probably just a guest from upstairs, though. I wouldn't want to cause any trouble."

"Miss Lacy, there are no guests right now. Mr. Doyle made sure you would have the place to yourself this week, to get the full effect." He winked when he said this and Lacy could see he was only half joking with her.

"Well, I believe I'm being spoiled. Thanks again, Howard."

"No trouble, dear. Your things will be up in a jiffy."

Chapter 5: Lucky Number Eight

Lacy thanked Howard, accepted the keys and an envelope with her name on it, which she assumed was the message he'd mentioned, and walked towards the stairs. Passing the chairs and the fireplace she was acutely aware of the sort of gravity possessed by superbly crafted furniture. She realized she was quite worn out from the trip and took her time walking up. The staircase curved to the right, supported by the ceiling over the check-in counter and landing on the second floor facing the opposite direction.

She found herself in front of another sitting area, beyond which she saw the French doors leading out to the balcony above the fountain. A long hallway led off to the right and left. There were several doors on either side, facing the front and rear of the house. The walls on this floor were bone white, punctuated with paintings between each door. Although too tired to give the art any serious consideration, Lacy could tell at a glance that they were museum quality. Each piece was well chosen, with soft colors that complemented the house and furniture; beautiful but not outlandish or loud in any way. Her shoes sank slightly into the thick, spongy maroon carpet, which cushioned and silenced her steps as she walked towards her room. *It's like walking on roses.*

Her key was a small fob, which activated a tiny, blinking green light when she waved it in front of the door knob. The knob turned easily and she found herself holding her breath as she pushed open the door. Her jaw dropped and she let out her breath with an unidentifiable "Ughhh!"

As part of Barbara's "research project", she had spent countless weekends in bed and breakfasts this past year, but nothing came close to this. The walls were a light lavender color; the wide planks of the hardwood floors were solid beneath her feet and gleamed with a freshly polished look. There were plush runners tracing a path from the bed to the bathroom in the opposite corner of the room. After surveying the room, her eyes drifted back to the bed; an enormous four-poster with a lace canopy. The heavy, velvet curtains on the window were a rich purple, deeper than the walls by a few shades. Pegged behind them was a second set of curtains, made of the same lace that draped the bed.

She walked to the window, breaking the privacy ensured by the lace and peeked out to view the estate. The extensive grounds were lit by globes of light on decorative posts and she could just make out a formal rose garden, a smaller kitchen garden, a number of gazebos, sitting areas and several topiaries. Beyond that, she could see the riding grounds, the stables, tennis courts and just a bit further, a line of dark blue that could only be the ocean. The canopy was drawn open on either side of the bed. Unable to resist any longer, Lacy flung herself backwards onto it. The bed was so welcoming she started to wonder if she'd had a couple glasses of champagne earlier and hadn't noticed. She almost couldn't feel the landing. *Perfect. Absolutely perfect...but I think I'm going to need a wakeup call tomorrow, or I might just stay right here the rest of the week.*

Two minutes later, just as she was beginning to question the necessity of a shower or if she should just crawl into the cloud beneath her, there was a soft tap on the door.

"Miss Stockton, it's me, Howard. We have your things here, if you're ready."

With a reluctant sigh, she forced herself to sit up and depart the fluff long enough to open the door. Standing aside she admitted a smiling Howard and an ecstatic Jonathan. *It's almost 9:30...don't they ever stop that smiling business?* Try as she might, the behavior was contagious and she felt herself caught up in their energy.

Jonathan carried her bags over to a chest of drawers on the side of the room, placing them on the rack beside it. Howard took a minute to walk Lacy around, pointing out a few of the "more necessary items," as he called them. There was stationery;

complete with her full name pre-printed on the sheets of paper, spa items in the bathroom, dried potpourri sprinkled about on the corners of the floor ("It's swept clear and changed daily, Miss, but if you would like a different blend, or none at all, say the word.") and more. Howard then gave her the rundown on the itinerary of the next day, while Jonathan turned down the bed.

"There will be a full breakfast served whenever you're ready, so please don't wake in a hurry, unless you're hungry. Even then don't forget about room service. The full menu is available, as well as special orders, if you require. Remember, I'm just downstairs if you should want anything at all."

"Thank you, Howard; I'm sure I'll be fine."

"Very well, Miss Stockton..."

"Excuse me?" she said with a mischievous grin.

"Very well, Miss *Lacy*. Jonathan reports that your car was just about full on fuel, but he did take the liberty of leaving some pamphlets and maps on the passenger seat, local attractions and such and don't forget, chef is more than happy to prepare picnic lunches. Everyone wants to ensure your comfort. And with that, I bid you good evening. Rest well."

"Thank you, gentlemen, this is great."

"Goodnight miss, we'll get the door."

As soon as the door shut, Lacy couldn't hear them. *Practically soundproof in here! Oh Barbara, you sneak! Now I see why you wouldn't tell me anything about this place ahead of time...*

Chapter 6: A Message

She walked into the bathroom and saw a hot bath waiting, complete with an assortment of oils, bath salts, even bubble bath, arranged on the corner of the tub. *That Jonathan is fast!* She glanced at the full-length mirror in the corner and peeled off her traveling jeans and top. The room was lit in a soft amber-rose color, reminiscent of morning sun through a stained-glass window, managing to be useful and flattering. *Why can't stores have lights like this in their dressing rooms?* She chose a floral-scented bath salt and sprinkled a handful of crystals into the water. Then, she settled into the tub and exhaled the rest of the tension out of her body. *Barbara would call this a small pool.*

Remembering her message, she reached over the side and grabbed her jeans. Drying her hands on the denim, she fished the envelope out of the rear pocket. *That woman works too hard...* As she eased back into the water, feeling the warmth glide around her shoulders like the soft hands of a masseuse, she smiled and opened the envelope. Beginning to read, she realized it wasn't from Barbara after all. The heavy, high-cotton cardstock felt smooth to her puckering fingertips. It was from Mr. Francis Doyle, in his own hand.

Dear Miss Stockton,

Please accept my sincerest apologies at not being able to greet you personally. I trust Howard has made you feel at home. It is our wish that you be very comfortable here at Haven. If you will forgive my absence, I would appreciate the chance to give you a more complete tour tomorrow afternoon. Please enjoy your evening. I will be able to meet with you, if you are available, at three, in the library.

Mrs. Livingston was kind enough to tell me a bit about you beforehand, so I have taken the opportunity to reserve Daredevil for you. I know you don't get many chances to ride in the city and I believe you will find him perfectly suited to you. Howard can direct you to the stables at your leisure. There are changing rooms available there. Forgive me for inquiring, but Mrs. Livingston was nice enough to volunteer your sizes and I have prepared a small wardrobe for you, including riding gear, which is waiting at the stables. If the sizes or styles do not suit you, do not hesitate to tell Pierre, the stable master, what you require. I look forward to meeting you.

Sincerely,

Frank Doyle

"Barbara! How could you?" she said aloud. Then she began to laugh heartedly and found herself becoming quite interested in meeting Mr. Doyle. He *appeared* an honest, caring, successful businessman and she never thought that string of words would be together in the same line. Barbara would definitely pay for sending along her sizes, but just thinking about a morning ride was enough to take the sting out of her embarrassment. She couldn't be sure, of course, but she had a pretty good idea that the clothes picked out for her would be a perfect fit.

How am I going to stop this guy's head from swelling? He needs to understand how lucky he is to win this award from a national publication! She almost couldn't help feeling like they were the lucky ones just for finding this place. *And how about that letter? Inviting, warm and carefully written...This man seems to know exactly what to say and how to say it...he must have had time to prepare for the arrival of the critic...*and although she would have liked to believe it, she had the feeling he would have done as much for any guest arriving at Haven.

After drying off and slipping into her favorite tank top and cotton bottoms, she climbed into the bed and almost immediately was feeling sleepy. *Do they drug the pillows here?* Just a wisp of excitement passed through her as she drifted off. *This is going to be interesting, that much is certain.*

Chapter 7: Morning Breaks

Lacy couldn't remember the last time she'd slept so deeply. The birds woke her a few minutes before the sun broke the horizon, but she had rested so well that she felt no malice towards their playful, happy chirping. Now, as the morning light sifted gracefully through the lace curtains, the thick down comforter was a maze of curled shadows. She lay there, catlike, soaking in the warmth and comfort. She had barely opened her eyes and there were already so many sensations to concentrate on. The glow of the sunlight evaporating the lavender sky, the weight of the comforter, the feeling that her body had been held aloft and healed overnight, now fully prepared for the day's activities. Then there were the smells; the dew on the grass, the fresh linens, and the floral potpourri scattered delicately about the room. She could even detect the scent of fresh bread coming from the kitchen downstairs.

"I don't think I'll ever get up..." she mused, opening her eyes to drink in the soft but clear light from the window. As if on cue, there was a soft knock at the door.

A small, female voice whispered from the hall, "Miss Stockton?"

"Yes? Come in?" she answered.

The door opened and a young woman, in her late teens, pushed a small cart into the room. Her bright almond eyes and delicately curled, dark hair appeared strangely exotic. Her small, slender frame seemed unlikely to control the cart so deftly, but she had no trouble maneuvering the wheels through the thick carpet in the hallway.

"How do you do, ma'am? My name is Cherice; I'll be your chambermaid. We thought you might like a little breakfast. Would you like me to draw you a bath?" Not waiting for an answer, Cherice pushed the cart quietly towards a small table by the door, stepped into the bathroom and quickly set the tub to fill.

Her mind still grasping at a number of sensations, Lacy managed to control her obvious lack of caffeine and smiled sweetly at the girl, thanking her. The girl curtsied, *actually curtsied* and left the room without another word. Lacy slipped into a thick, soft, white robe that had somehow materialized on the far corner of the bed.

On the cart, under the shining, silver domes, were an assortment of bite-sized, fresh-baked herbal and sweet breads, zeppoli and homemade donuts, strawberries so big that Lacy could barely take a bite without cutting them in half first and other delicacies. A small French press of strong coffee, a crystal carafe of fresh-squeezed orange juice and a half-sized bottle of Champagne stood at attention next to her plate.

I could seriously get used to this, she thought, as she eased herself into the bath with a cup of coffee in one hand and one of the enormous strawberries in the other. The bath was the perfect temperature, of course. She noticed a small, digital screen on the wall and after some consideration and a few sips of coffee, she understood it to be a touch screen temperature gauge for the tub. *I'm in a giant hotpot!* She smiled and settled back, not sure what time it was and not sure she wanted to know.

After a delicious bath and breakfast, she dressed in jeans and a light top and walked downstairs. It would have been easy to choose one of the books from the shelf in the hall and get back into bed, but that date with Daredevil was something she did not plan on missing.

"Ah, Miss Stockton," came a familiar voice.

"Howard, you promised..." she replied with false sincerity.

"I meant, good morning, *Miss Lacy*. How did you sleep?"

"That's much better. Howard, I believe I slept better last night then I have in the past six years, at least. But you were here late last night. Pulling an early shift this morning as well?"

"Well, we all help each other out around here, Miss Lacy. And I wanted to make sure you were on your way to your morning ride...Cherice didn't wake you I trust?"

"She was an angel of mercy, Howard. Had my bath drawn and food in my face before I even realized I was awake!" He smiled at this and came out from around the counter, with a paper in his hand.

"Glad to hear it, she is a special girl. This is a map of the grounds. If you'll head down that hall, through the restaurant and out the back door, it's the quickest way to the stables. Pierre will have your things waiting. You have a good time now."

"Thank you, Howard; I'm sure that won't be difficult." She took the map and headed off down the hall. This hall mirrored the second floor, with tasteful, comforting art mounted at regular intervals; only the color scheme was different. The walls were a soft yellow, with white frames for the art work and around the doors.

She passed a library, ballroom and another small sitting room before finding herself in the long, bright dining area. Small clusters of tables and chairs were spread carefully throughout the space, which was light and airy. The entire rear wall was composed of French doors and large windows, stretching to the ceiling.

She walked through the deserted restaurant, looking out the windows at the extensive grounds and terraced gardens, coming to a pair of doors, pegged open unlike the rest.

Stepping through the doors, she heard a grandfather clock chiming from next to the podium at the front of the restaurant. She stopped momentarily, listening to the clock play its calming melody and counted the soft strikes until they stopped at eight. *Eight a.m. and I feel like I slept for two days! I still have plenty of time to ride.*

Once she crossed the threshold onto the brick patio, she was met with the scent of jasmine, dewy moisture and fresh cut grass. Blinking to adjust to the sunlight, she glanced at the map, chose the walkway leading south and strolled along the path, breathing deep in the morning air.

As she walked she admired the flowers planted along the walkway, the glimpse of gardens off across the lawn, the spectacle of gazebos and sitting areas in the shade of mature oak and walnut trees. After several minutes, she came to a large, white, barn-like building which she took to be the stables.

Chapter 8: Daredevil

Taking another glance around, she saw that each shrub, tree, terrace and landmark was placed in such a way as to seem a permanent part of the landscape; nature and man working together to create a harmonious space. An environment crafted for the comfort of the mind and soul. The sight of two horseshoes, mounted facing up, above the open stable doors reminded her that she would have to postpone studying the grounds in detail until later.

Her face was flushed with the cool morning air; chills ran through her as she realized in just a few minutes she'd be riding through the wild, wooded areas behind the stable. Walking into the shaded interior of the structure, the smell of fresh hay and moisture in the air, she saw a magnificent stallion, with a coat like onyx, standing in the center of the stable. She froze. The stallion looked at her, intense intelligence behind his eyes. He dipped and raised his head slowly, standing with confidence and looking past her at the grounds towards the inn.

"I hope he hasn't startled you, Miss. Daredevil won't hurt you. He's actually excited to see you. He could tell something was going on this morning." The soft voice came from the darkness to the left of the horse. A handsome young man of about twenty-five, medium build, dark-haired with olive skin, stepped out towards the horse. His hand calmly traced a path along the beast's back and neck, coming to rest on the bridle. "Miss Stockton, I presume?"

Lacy nodded, still frozen in her steps, but more out of wonder than fear.

"What a beautiful animal. What...a *beautiful* horse," she said, slowly stepping forward. The horse bowed its head down towards her, approving of her scent and allowing her to pat its forehead, neck and shoulder.

"Yes, Daredevil's truly a special stallion. He was raised here from birth, he knows every inch of the grounds and he has a spirit in him that is stronger than that of any horse I've known and I've known many. If you don't mind me saying so ma'am, I think he approves of you. If you'll step into that changing room behind you, I'll saddle him up." Pierre gestured to the wall opposite the stables, which was made up of a line of doors, each apparently a small bungalow for changing and the storage of riding gear.

"Yes, thank you Pierre." He bowed slightly at the mention of his name and she walked off, turning once more to gaze at the horse. The horse returned her look, matching her desire to run, to feel the land pound beneath them. He seemed eager to be on their way.

She wasn't surprised to find the clothes fit perfectly. The fact that her host knew enough about her size to see that the tan, skin-tight riding pants were a flattering fit made her feel a little embarrassed. She changed quickly, stepping out of the bungalow to see Daredevil waiting, *alone*, in the sunlight at the door of the stable. He watched her walk towards him, whinnying impatiently when she looked around for Pierre, finally stepping towards her when she hesitated to close the distance between them. She smiled, went alongside him and mounted; settling herself into his polished, black saddle. She leaned down, put her arms around his neck and whispered into his ear, "OK, Daredevil, show me your home..."

With joint cries of delight, they were off, out of the stable grounds and into the land behind the buildings. The horse anticipated her commands, seemed to mold to her physically, the two of them becoming one mighty beast, galloping through streams, across small fields, even leaping boulders. They coursed through the trees, fearless and full of wind and light.

After several minutes they came to a secluded glen, with a trickle of a stream coursing through it. Lacy lightened her grip on the reins and the horse slowly stepped through the shafts of morning light and mist, taking a drink from the clear water of the stream. She looked around, breathing heavy, appreciating the few moments of peace. Leaning over to wrap her arms around Daredevil's muscular neck, she rested her head on him, watching sideways as the dragonflies danced on the wildflowers growing on the sloped embankment. A content sigh poured out of her and the horse seemed to echo it with a snorting, weighty exhale of its own.

When they returned to the stable, Lacy was not surprised to find her eyes tearing. *I could say it was the wind*...she thought, but she knew the journey she had just been on was much more than a casual ride in the country. Pierre was waiting by the stable door. He looked at her flushed face, at the tears on her cheeks. Offering his hand to help her out of the saddle, he handed her a small towel, smiling knowingly. The mighty horse nodded a few times before allowing Pierre to take the reins and walk him off to be brushed down.

"Thank you Pierre! Thank you Daredevil!" she called out, trying to keep her voice from cracking with emotion.

As man and horse walked off into the darker area of the stable, Pierre waved his hand. "I'll have him ready for you tomorrow morning, Miss Stockton," he called over his shoulder.

Smiling, she collected her things from the bungalow and walked towards the inn, ready for a quick shower and a better look around.

Chapter 9: Caught Unaware

"Barbara, you wouldn't believe this place! Our readers will think they've died and gone to heaven!" Lacy spoke into her cell phone, as she slowly wandered through the halls of the second floor. The artwork on the walls demanded closer scrutiny, but a call from her boss and best friend was a welcome interlude.

"Lacy, darling, I know the place is incredible, but have you met the man yet?" Barbara did not hide the mischief in her voice very well.

"Not yet, but I just had the most amazing ride through some of the grounds! I'm supposed to meet the big boss this afternoon. I might have met him briefly the other night, but if that was him I think I'd rather concentrate on the inn..."

"I don't think that was him, Lacy. You'll know when you meet him, believe me. Oh...and um...keep your eyes open around there, hon. Something strange is going on at Haven." Barbara actually sounded serious for once.

"What do you mean, *something strange*?"

"No one seems to be quite sure, that's what I mean. But Mr. Doyle has a lot of friends in high places and it seems that whatever is going on around there is going to continue. It may not even have anything to do with him, it might be something his mother started when she was helping out more, I don't know. Just keep your eyes open."

"I will, thanks for checking up on me and thanks for the convertible, I can't wait to prowl the streets of that adorable town in it."

"Yeah, yeah, don't thank me; just write me a damn good cover story!" Barbara burst into one of her sonnets of laughter, to which Lacy added her own refrain before hanging up to go downstairs to the restaurant.

Lunch consisted of shrimp scampi with handmade fettuccine, followed by the biggest slice of double-chocolate cake she had ever seen. She managed a few tempting bites before having the waiter clear the table. Once she was finished, it was all she could do to stride slowly down the hall and settle into one of the cozy, leather chairs in the library. She actually dozed off for a few moments, a copy of the February issue of House To Home across her lap.

After her ride, a quick shower had deposited her into a lightweight, white sundress that fell to about an inch above the knee, with a little ripple along the bottom. With her legs raised on a footrest nearby, her dress had slipped up several inches, leaving her lower thighs exposed. As she awoke she noticed her bare legs in front of her and casually reached down to smooth out her skirt. When she did so, she heard a man's voice coming from the door.

"I was rather hoping you wouldn't do that..."

Lacy froze. Then she finished smoothing her skirt, tucked her legs under her as gracefully as she could and stood up. Turning to face the man to whom the voice belonged, she saw he was smiling roguishly and felt her face redden. She tried not to smile back, but did not succeed. His face had a boy-like charm. They both chuckled and he spoke again, his voice calm and soft, which only made her strain to listen harder.

"I'm sorry if I startled you, but you looked so cozy, I didn't want to wake you. My name is Francis Doyle, but I would like it very much if you called me Frank." He stepped forward and offered his hand to the still somewhat dazed Lacy.

"Nice to meet you, I'm Lacy Stockton, from House to Home magazine. I'm sorry if I missed our appointment, I must have dozed off for a few moments..."

"Say nothing of it, I'm actually early. I've been looking forward to meeting you. I hope you've enjoyed your stay?"

"Yes, very much. I can see why you won our highest award, you certainly know charming, I mean, I mean everything is so luxurious and inviting...and that...I've enjoyed my stay very much." *Nice one, Lace! Just don't look at him! Walk out the door without looking at him!*

"I've tried very hard to make Haven a place to recuperate the soul, as well as the mind and body. I'm pleased to hear that you're not disappointed." *There's that smile again, don't look at it!* But she did look. In fact, she felt like she couldn't take her eyes off him! His dark hair fell casually across his forehead. His skin was a healthy bronze color and was wrapped around his sporty physique without any looseness visible. His wide smile projected so much warmth and charisma; Lacy could just imagine what it would be like to hear him speak to a crowd. But it was the eyes that did it. Light blue, like topaz; sparkling with joy, but also mysterious. Yes, there was much more to Mr. Doyle than met the eye. For a few seconds of rushing blood and awkwardness, they looked deeply into each other's eyes, squeezing close together to step through the door. Then Lacy caught herself.

"I wanted to thank you, Frank, for allowing me to ride Daredevil. He's magnificent."

"You're welcome; Pierre told me you rode like you were made for each other. I'm glad. I'm afraid I don't have the time to take him out for much of a run anymore and I never allow the guests near him." He smiled and they locked gazes again, "I just knew you'd be...different. I'm very happy to find I was right." He looked down, almost shy for a moment. After the pause, when his eyes glanced back to hers, they had altered somehow. They were colder, harder and businesslike; but Lacy got the feeling that the subtle anger, which seemed to dwell behind them, was not directed at her. When he spoke again, his voice was soft, reassuring her that she was correct. "I'm sorry to say that the reason I was early is because I need to postpone our meeting. Some rather urgent business has come up and I must attend to it. However, if you would join me for dinner, I would very much enjoy seeing you this evening to make up for it."

"I think I would like that."

The smile came back full force, or maybe it had never left? Lacy wasn't sure. Her head was spinning with the desire to know this man, to discover what was behind those eyes. He spoke again, "I'll meet you in the restaurant, shall we say eight o'clock?"

"Sounds lovely."

"See you then." He strode off quickly. Could he have actually been nervous about her answer? Whatever he was, Lacy was sure about one thing; she was definitely not going to be late tonight. She turned and walked back to the lobby, drifted upstairs and into her room, falling backwards onto the bed. *Next time we meet, Mr. Doyle, I will be more prepared!* She chuckled as she thought of her embarrassment at being found asleep. She tried to think of the gardens she would have to cover that afternoon, the notes she would take, how it would all fit into the cover story somehow, but she kept coming back to the image of his smile. *"I just knew you'd be different." Hmmm...And the normal guests don't ride Daredevil? I think I'm at a disadvantage here.*

With a mischievous smile of her own, she thought of the black dress she had hanging in the closet. There are things, she knew, that a woman could do to turn the tide. She grabbed her notepad and sunglasses and walked out of the room, heading to the gardens. As she stepped outside, her thoughts turned to the intense look his eyes held as he was mentioning the "urgent business" he had to cancel her tour for. *Barbara's right, something is going on around here.* She felt a flush of excitement thinking how she might be the one to find out exactly what that was.

Chapter 10: Dinner at Eight

It took every bit of willpower she had to wait in the library until a few minutes after eight. Then she found herself rushing down the darkened hall to the restaurant. The entire ground floor seemed deserted and the restaurant was quite dark. At first, Lacy thought perhaps his "urgent business" had lasted longer than he had planned. Then she noticed one table in the center of the restaurant that had a small oil lamp burning on it. As she walked towards it, she saw a white, embossed card that read *"Reserved."*
Smiling, she wondered if she should sit down, when she noticed a note card on one of the plates. In the light of the oil lamp, she read, *"I'm in the kitchen. Frank."*

She turned and walked towards the double-swing doors, curiosity forcing a nervous, questioning smile to her lips. As she walked into the brightly lit, stainless steel and white tile kitchen, she saw Frank standing with his back to her in front of one of the massive, eight burner stoves. He turned his head, eyebrows shooting up in surprise. He looked her over, head-to-toe and back again to her eyes. "Wow," he smiled. "You could certainly be a dangerous distraction in the kitchen. Please come in."

She glanced down at the flowing trip on her black dress and at his sharp black tuxedo. When her eyes met his with a questioning look, he smiled and gestured towards a chrome and black stool on the other side of the island. "I gave the cook the night off, hope you don't mind homemade dishes. I wanted us to be able to spend some time together, without interruption."

"Do you always cook in a tuxedo? I would have dressed more appropriately if I knew...I certainly wouldn't mind helping."

"No, no. I wouldn't change the way you were dressed for the deed to the town! I rarely get a chance to cook for anyone; I truly enjoy it. Have a seat."

She sat on the stool and watched him, feeling somewhat childish. His hands moved quickly, flowing across the tasks he was performing. He held the knife with confidence and moved with practiced skill.

"You cook, too?" Lacy asked. "Where do you find the time?"

"This is something my mother taught me. I spent much of my childhood in a stool like that one, just watching." With this he smiled impishly and flipping the knife, shot a small piece of cucumber arching into the air towards her face. Surprised, but not about to let him catch her off guard, she leaned back and caught it in her mouth. They both doubled over in laughter. "I see you have hidden talents as well...glad you're not allergic!" he said, when they had caught their breath.

"Mr. Doyle, you have no idea..." she smiled. "So what are you making us? It smells delicious." The kitchen was flooded with the scent of bacon, garlic, onions and spices she didn't recognize. She hoped her stomach wasn't going to voice its enthusiasm as well.

"An old family recipe, Pasta Carbonara," he said, pausing with the knife long enough to put his hand over his heart. "Guaranteed to melt your heart...or give you heartburn, anyway. Do you like Italian?"

"Mmm...Italian...and homemade. That's very romantic. Do you always mix business and pleasure?" She flashed her most alluring smile.

"Miss Stockton, when you own an inn, you're your business *is* pleasure." They laughed again at this. He continued to cook, she continued to flirt. After, when they took the prepared food to the restaurant, they talked about the region, how long he'd been in New Hampshire and where she was born. Their gaze drifted along each other's features from across the little table. After the effects of wine, candles, good food and good conversation, he caught her eyes with his and held them for a few seconds of silence. "I should get you into bed." Catching her comedic look, he corrected it with, "I mean of course, allow me to walk you to your room, Miss Stockton."

"Why yes, that would be nice." She smiled and they walked quietly through the halls. Catching herself feeling playfully nervous, she stole glances at him, in an attempt to measure his intentions. All too quickly it seemed to her, they reached her door. They turned and he took her hand in his. It was the first time they had touched that night. His hand was warm and held hers like it was an egg, cautious, firm and protective.

"Lacy, I want you to know that this has been a rare treat for me. I'm a busy man and I don't often get the chance to spend time with a lovely lady. I am not just saying this for a good review; I'm truly enjoying myself. Thank you for seeing me this evening."

"I'm very happy you asked me to join you. This whole trip has been like something out of a dream. I've had the most wonderful time. I'm glad you could meet me...I was a bit worried this afternoon when you were called away. Everything go all right?"

The hard eyes returned, "Everything went fine. I don't think I'll need to cancel again." The eyes softened a bit and turned back to meet hers. "In fact, I'd like to offer you a proper tour of West Dobley tomorrow, if you'd like?"

"I think I would truly enjoy that, thank you. And thank you for cooking, it was delicious." *I can't believe I want him to kiss me on the first date!* She paused and they looked into each other's eyes. He moved in towards her, just a fraction of an inch, hovering above her upturned face. But then he stopped, glanced toward the floor briefly before meeting her eyes again. The broad, playful smile returned full-force and in a sudden, deft movement, he stepped back, and raised her hand to his lips to kiss it.

She burst into a relieved, familiar chuckle, saying, "Why thank you!" and giving a small curtsy. It was a fun and welcome end to the night, after the misplaced, awkward scenes she had been a part of with other men. However, the laughter and tension breaker didn't quite distract her from noticing that strange look in his eyes, like he was consciously clouding his thoughts from her, hiding something, or holding something back.

"No, thank *you*. I will be by after your morning ride, maybe...around eleven?"

"I will be waiting, Frank."

"Good night, Lacy."

"Good night." She smiled as he stepped away and then she turned and shut the door. As soon as she shut it, she peered through the peephole and watched him. He stood there in the hall, hesitating, looking down. Then, with a quick shake of his head, he walked off down the hall.

She fell on the bed, the warmth of the wine and the excitement of the evening coursed through her veins and combined, leaving her cozy and thrilled at the same time. *How am I supposed to sleep tonight? I feel like I'm in a movie!*

She shot off a quick text to Barbara, "Wow."

A few minutes later her phone buzzed and she read Barbara's reply, "Wow? What wow?? Did you meet him?? What's the wow??"

"Just...wow," she answered, laughing as she imagined her friend's face. *She could use a bit of her mysterious maneuvers dished back to her anyway.* With an audible "Humph!" she casually shut her phone off.

After rinsing off quickly, she squeezed her hair into a towel, pulled back the sheets and got into bed. Laying perfectly still and yet feeling slightly dizzy, she shut the light and stared at the ceiling. *One heck of an assignment...am I dreaming?* She lay there a few minutes, until gradually her body succumbed to the comfort of the bed and she closed her eyes. As she was drifting off, she saw his smiling face in her mind. It hovered close to hers, leaning in, only this time he didn't pull away, didn't even hesitate. He kissed her warmly and tenderly and she fell asleep in his phantom arms.

Chapter 11: A Compliment

She awoke early again the next morning, totally recharged. Daredevil was ready as always and waiting in the stable. "Daredevil, I'm nervous!" she spoke, before climbing on. The horse shook its head up and down, lightly pawing the ground as if in acknowledgement. Whether he understood or not, Lacy knew he'd do his best to make her ride a thrilling escape from whatever tension she carried with her. After traveling over fields of wildflowers, cold, rushing streams, lazy, quiet forests and hilltops bright with the morning sun, they stopped at their hideaway before returning to the stables. She felt refreshed and grateful. *That was just what I needed...* She gave the horse a carrot from the feed bins and left him in Pierre's care.

Walking back to the inn, she glanced at the sun. Upon reaching the patio the grandfather clock in the dining area confirmed what she had guessed; it was still early. *Not even nine yet! Does time stop here?* The ride had shook most of the nerves out, but reaching for the door handle some of them flickered a triumphant return. The butterflies in her stomach had not fluttered like this since prom. She smiled as she thought this, especially when she remembered her date. She had always been drawn to the type of man who would treat her badly. She used to think men signed a contract somewhere that if they met Lacy Stockton, they had to treat her like dirt or be banished forever from the human race. Come to think of it, most of the men she dated seemed like they must have suffered that punishment before meeting her.

But Frank is different, isn't he? Courteous, professional, sensitive and strong, fun to be with... There was no question he was handsome and yes, definitely sexy. Flushed from the ride and her train of thought, she took the stairs in a hurry, hoping to get to her room and her bathtub, before being discovered. No such luck. Almost like she had been waiting for her to return, Cherice stood patiently by her bedroom door, an enormous smile on her face. Lacy found herself smiling back.

"Good morning, Miss Stockton! The morning agrees with you, you look beautiful, like you have soaked up all sunshine!"

"Thank you, Cherice! Come on in. I just came from riding." She unlocked the door and Cherice followed her in timidly. Lacy could feel her eyes on her back as she walked into the bathroom and grabbed a towel to wipe her face. "Cherice, your service borders on paranoia. It's only nine in the morning."

"I'm sorry ma'am...I just...I wanted to make sure you had everything you wanted."

Lacy saw her eyes go to the floor and walked closer. When she straightened up, she locked gazes with her. "What's up, Cherice? What's wrong?"

"It's nothing. I'm being silly. What can I bring you?"

"Cherice..."

"Honestly, miss. I'm imposing."

"Cherice, out with it! Don't get me confused with the normal clientele around here. Now what's up?"

"Miss Lacy, I'm sorry...I just...I want to know how you do that?"

"Do what, hon?"

"How you look so nice all the time. You always seem to know who you are and where you're going. I've never seen anyone so beautiful, Miss Lacy and that's the honest truth."

She's emulating me? This sweet child is actually impressed! "Thank you for saying so, Cherice. But I certainly don't feel that way, not all the time at least. How old are you?"

"I'm eighteen, miss."

"Well, Cherice. I don't agree with your assessment one hundred percent; in fact I feel I have a long way to go sometimes. But I will tell you something. Some things you can only learn when you are forced to learn them. I hate to say it, but most of life is like that, you go through it and when it gets tough, you learn a little and hurt a little and move on. But you are a beautiful, intelligent, young woman. You have a big heart and a good soul and that's some of the most important things you'll need. The only other thing you need to remember is that you are special and no one has the right to make you feel anything other than that. If they do, they're not worth your time." She wanted to sound like Barbara and hoped her own insecurities and dating failures didn't show on her face as she provided this advice.

Cherice was quiet for a while, smiling and thinking about what Lacy had said, tears slowly filling her eyes until one or two spilled over the edge. "Thank you, Miss Stockton. That means a lot."

"Cherice, if we are going to be friends and I certainly hope we are, you are going to need to start calling me Lacy. Got it?"

Laughing now, Cherice came towards her and began to shake her hand with great vigor. "Ok, *Miss*

Lacy. Thank you. I wish you would never have to leave Haven. You make it so nice here!"

"Cherice, sometimes I think I won't be able to leave, even when they want me to!"

They both laughed at this and Cherice disappeared into the bathroom to fill the bath, then left, saying she would bring breakfast in a bit. Lacy smiled back, hoping she had done something to strengthen Cherice. She vaguely remembered her mom having a talk with her much like that when she was about Cherice's age and Barbara *still* talked like that. *Cherice, if I can help you half as much as that woman helps me, you'll be just fine.*

Chapter 12: Let's Take a Ride

After yet another luxurious bath and the promised breakfast, it was a little after ten. Standing in front of her closet, she wavered indecisively between a few outfits, finally choosing some khaki Capri's, a white tank top and light, gauzy blouse and a red and white striped silk scarf. Looking in the full-length mirror while she slipped into sandals, she did a half twirl. With a mischievous grin, she thought of the red convertible waiting downstairs and whispered to herself, "Hold on to your socks, Mr. Doyle."

She was still early by about ten minutes, so she walked downstairs and greeted Howard. He mentioned how charming she looked for a "day in the country," and promised to have one of the boys bring the convertible around. She sat on the front steps, sunglasses on, soaking up the sun. Her watch read eleven, on the dot. As if on cue, the car pulled up, shining in the sunlight and beaming with the recent wash and wax it had obviously been given. It was driven by another well-dressed young man, who introduced himself as Charles, stepped out and asked if he should put the top down. She thanked him and leaned against the car, her hands on the hood.

The front doors opened and Frank Doyle walked out. She was happy to see that he looked as good in casual dress as he had the other night in his tux. Actually, he seemed more approachable, even *snuggly!* He wore thick khaki trousers, a maroon polo jersey, sandals and sunglasses. He carried a basket, which Lacy knew would be full of delightful delicacies. He also wore an enormous smile, which Lacy donned as well.

"Good morning, Mr. Doyle...You ready for me?" Lacy asked, smacking the hood of the convertible with one hand and pulling the scarf from her neck to tie around her hair.

"I made sure I got enough rest, Miss Stockton, thank you. You driving?" He made his way towards the car and slipped the basket into the back seat, then turned towards the young man standing next to the driver door. Charles stood there, transfixed, holding the door open and fixated on the intricacies of Lacy's scarf tying. "That will be all, thank you Charles...Charles?"

"Huh? Oh! Yes sir, thank you sir. Have a good day ma'am!" He smiled and stepped away from the car to assume his position by the door.

"I think you have bewitched our doorman, *ma'am.*" He said to Lacy as she laughed and slipped into the driver's seat. *Let's hope it's contagious,* she thought.

Putting the car in gear, she launched down the driveway, drawing laughter from Charles at the door and chuckles coupled with quick grasps at the seatbelt from Frank.

Chapter 13: A Quiet Surprise

With Lacy at the wheel and Frank navigating, they found the highway and cruised along in the sun and the wind. The shady, hunter green mass of trees on one side of the road contrasted sharply with the rocky cliffs crashing into a blue-gray Atlantic on the other. Frank pointed out some of the natural scenery and they laughed, sharing stories of adventures from their youth. Catching a minute of silence, he turned, looking at her profile, following the line of her body in the sunlight, down to her legs and back up to her hair blowing in the wind.

"Thank you for seeing me today. I'm glad you weren't too sick from dinner last night..."

"Thank you for asking me out, Frank. Dinner was fabulous, but I thought you might be too busy to spend any more time with me. I'm happy to see I was wrong...so where are we going?"

"It's a surprise."

"Oh, the handsome stranger abducts the heroine and carries her off to *zee casbah, no?*"

"Well, that was sort of the plan...you shook things up a bit when you decided to drive...but I'm glad you did. It gives me time to look at you."

Lacy's smile couldn't have been bigger if her head were full of teeth. *Thank you, Barbara! Thank you, thank you, thank you!*

"You know, I never would have admitted it, I'm more of a city girl, but you seem to have found paradise here, this place is gorgeous. Is there a catch?"

"Yeah, it's called winter. But even that is bearable if...you stay warm enough."

Frank told her to slow the car and turn off the highway at the next exit, which was more of a break in the trees than anything else. They pulled onto a dirt road, which had a bar across it with a padlock securing it in place.

"Hmmm...seems like your plan was foiled, Mr. Doyle. Somebody doesn't want us in there..."

"But my dear Miss Stockton, that somebody, is *me.*" Stepping out of the car, Frank pulled a keyring from his pocket and unlocked the gate. Drawing it aside he bowed and gestured towards the road ahead. Lacy made a revving motion on the steering wheel and the car lurched through the gate, kicking up a small whirlwind of dust.

Laughing, Frank swung the gate shut, leaving it unlocked and hopped back into the car. Lacy meandered, a bit more cautiously, up the narrow, uneven road. Large trees, like parasols, shaded the road and Lacy realized she could no longer hear any highway traffic. All she could hear was birds chirping and small animals scurrying in the woods all around. She continued driving slowly, half afraid that some small, furry thing would jump in front of the car. The road was uphill all the way.

Noticing her caution, Frank smiled, saying, "Don't worry, the little ones will get out of the way, just keep an eye out for the bears..."

"Bears?!" Lacy flashed him a worried glance, quickly turning her eyes back to the road and woods with renewed caution, until she heard Frank laughing. She took one hand off the wheel long enough to backhand his shoulder, while he faked a blocking motion and continued to laugh. After a few minutes, they came to a clearing, the top of the hill, where she saw what appeared to be a small cabin standing in the sunlight.

"This is my hideaway. Come on!" He leaped out of the car and grabbed the basket from the back seat.

Lacy raised an eyebrow, but got out of the car and followed him up to the steps. "So is this where you bring your maidens to deflower?"

"Only the ones dumb enough to get in the car...come on in."

Following him inside, she saw the cabin was very clean, very cozy and full of light. What she had seen from the driveway was apparently the backside. Once she walked in the door, it was clear that the structure was positioned to face the view on the other side of the property. Skylights on the cathedral ceiling let sun in from above, while the wall directly ahead was constructed of large windows, thick, cedar beams and a row of French doors, similar to the dining room at the inn, except that here they showed a view of the coastline for miles.

Glancing around the open floor plan, she saw large, simple, comfortable furniture in the sunken living area, the well equipped kitchen off to one side and stairs that lead to a loft hallway. It was much bigger than it looked from the drive up. She guessed several bedrooms were tucked behind those doors. Lacy got the feeling that this was someplace he came quite often.

"This is beautiful, Frank."

"I'm glad you like it. The truth is I was a little nervous; I've never actually brought anyone here. My mother visits this place once in a while, but not much lately. I don't let the staff near it; they're busy enough with Haven. So it's sort of my own space, take it or leave it." She couldn't imagine anyone leaving it. He finished emptying the basket onto the counter, taking out a bottle and putting it in an ice bucket. "This will take a few minutes to cool down; come on, I want to show you something."

He walked out the French doors, pinning them open with his foot and flicking the ceiling fans on by a switch on the wall. He took her hand and walked her out to one side of a large sundeck. She felt a slight flutter at his touch and in anticipation of the view. At this time of day, the house blocked the direct sun from this part of the deck, so she lifted her sunglasses from her eyes and looked out where he was pointing. Away in the distance, past the beautiful coastline, she saw a cluster of buildings, noting one bright, white one in particular, alone on a hill of green. She heard the surf pounding below, the rhythm almost hypnotic and each wave bringing along a gust of fresh, sea air.

"When I was a kid, mom would take us up here, sort of camping. Dad was...not with us usually. She always loved this place. She said this was what life should be like. Haven was just a rundown version of itself, surrounded by acres of trees and little else. Mom always said it was too much land for one building. She used to dream of a little town, perfect in every way, off down the coast. When I was older, after I was successful in several smaller ventures, I came and built her a cabin here. Then I proceeded to build her the town."

Suddenly she realized what she was looking at, off in the distance. "Frank! Do you mean that West Dobley is...yours?"

"Almost entirely. It took several years, a lot of palm pressing and a lot of restless nights. Tenants and managers are allowed to purchase small percentages, as a profit sharing plan, but I maintain the largest shareholder by a very wide margin. It would have been quicker and easier with more investors, but it wouldn't have been right. They always want to cut corners and are more interested in profit than quality. I found many willing investors that had money but lacked vision. When I was a kid there was nothing but a highway and the surf down that coastline. I like to think we improved on that, by giving this stretch of highway something worth traveling to. So yes, West Dobley is mostly mine. Mine and Mom's. She had a lot of input."

"Wow. That's some present. Does your Mom live in the town?"

"Not always. She spends a lot of time away on projects, but comes back whenever she can. She does love it."

"I should say so!" Looking out over the town hugging the coastline, she thought of the multitude of streets and buildings, the private police force and Haven, of course, the jewel in the crown. Lacy was in awe. Suddenly she felt very small. Here was a man who had dedicated his life to building something, creating an entire atmosphere of comfort, luxury, service and beauty. She realized at that moment whatever happened with the remainder of the week didn't matter all that much. She felt open, like she had grown somehow. She realized that all week she had been inspired and pampered and had stopped thinking so much about her problems, her faults. Almost overcome with emotion, she felt her eyes shining.

Sensing something had shifted, Frank turned towards her. "What is it, Lacy? What's wrong? I hope that didn't sound like bragging, I certainly didn't mean it to. I just wanted your readers to see the real me. And to understand that it's a lot of hard work and sacrifice to follow your dreams, but that it can be worth it."

"Nothing's wrong, Frank. You've really done something special. It's a rare gift to make things happen that change people. There's a lot of money being thrown around New York, but not many do something this constructive with it. This trip has already been so much more than a job to me. I feel...I feel different, better somehow, then when I came here. I can't explain it, but I want to thank you for it."

She looked down and felt Frank's arms circle gently around her. Although she had never been described as "touchy-feely," she felt herself melt into his chest, her own arms circling around him. "I couldn't ask for higher praise than that. Thank you, Lacy," he said quietly. They stood like that for a moment, until he released her and stood back, smiling. Handing her a handkerchief from his back pocket, he said, "I could use a drink. Champagne?"

"Definitely!" she answered, laughing a little at her emotional response and following him into the cabin. He went to the kitchen and she collapsed into the sofa, hugging a pillow.

Chapter 14: Time Flies

After a few minutes she heard the cork pop quietly and he appeared with the bottle in one hand and two glasses in the other. He handed one to her, filled it, filled the other and tasted it. Setting it down on the coffee table, he disappeared again, only to reappear with a tray of sandwiches and small crocks of soup.

Suddenly realizing she was hungry, Lacy put the pillow aside and grabbed a sandwich. It was a large, crusty roll, piled high with meats and cheeses. Frank looked on with amusement while she managed to fit a small corner of the sandwich into her mouth and bite down. "Maybe I should have had them make something a bit more bite size..."

"No!" she said between chewing motions, "it's delicious! And I'm starving!"

He laughed and grabbed a sandwich himself. After they had eaten and talked and relaxed and talked some more, Frank turned to her and said, "I'd better be getting you back, you have a reputation to uphold..."

Smiling, Lacy sat up to glance at her watch. *Six-thirty! I can't believe we've been here, talking, all day!* "I had no idea it was so late! Time flies when you're..."

"Having fun..." they laughed and caught each other's gaze. "I'm sorry if we never made it to the town...I wanted to show you this place and have some time to talk."

"I'm really glad you did. I can check out the town tomorrow. Besides, I prefer to see it on my own, in order to keep my *journalistic integrity* intact." She winked at this. "...but I think I may have to leave this cabin out of the article. Wouldn't want my readers to get the wrong idea..."

Frank smiled at her joke, but she could sense him withdrawing. Once again she got the feeling there was more going on then he wanted to share. And again, he seemed to catch himself and look back to her eyes with a smile. "You can have the town to yourself tomorrow on one condition; I request your presence back at Haven around eight, for dinner. And I'd like your input on the party..."

"The party?"

"Well, the magazine wanted to throw us a party...to celebrate the award. Only I couldn't see the sense of having a bunch of rich people slapping me on the back for making an inn that most people can't afford to stay in for more than a night or two. So I told them I'd go through with it on two conditions; one, it's on my dime. And two; that we make it more than a celebration about the award, so we're going to do it as a fundraiser for a good cause..."

"Like a shelter for women in need or something?" She smiled, meaning it as a joke to check his reaction, but she could see a slight bewilderment flash across his face.

"Exactly."

"Well that sounds great, Frank. Let me know if there's anything I can do to help, but you have to do a favor for me..."

"Your wish is my command. What is it?"

"Drive us home? I'm much too relaxed to navigate that dirt road downhill and dodge any bears that pop up. With dusk on the way and all."

"Done." He was smiling now.

"Besides," she added as they locked the door to the cabin and turned towards the car, "it will give me a chance to look *at you*."

Frank laughed again and, opening the door for her, accepted the keys, echoing her earlier statement with a mischievous grin of his own, "Anything *I* can do to help..."

They drove back to Haven, the roof still down, but the heater blowing lightly, as the evening had grown cool. They pulled into the driveway just as the sun was setting and the stars coming out. Howard was waiting on the steps with a worried look on his face. As they pulled up, Frank took her hand in both of his, thanked her again for coming and then turned to Howard. As they walked off around the corner towards the garage of the house, Frank turned back to wave goodnight and Lacy waved back. Then she walked through the door and up the stairs to her room, the blood in her ears like a tiny surf crashing in her head. She knew she had a lot to write down tonight, with all the character reference material she was now in possession of; there would be no sleep for a while.

Chapter 15: The Silence is Broken

Lacy awoke with a start, sitting up in bed. Even with the ability of the carpet and doors to muffle sound, she heard a loud banging and several voices shouting. She grabbed her robe and rushed downstairs. When she reached the lobby, she saw Howard. He had a worried look on his face, standing behind the closed front door, furiously speaking into a walkie-talkie. She couldn't make out much of what was said in the commotion, but thought she heard, "Take him down! Take him down, now! Police are en route!"

Then she heard the heavy footsteps of Frank coming from the back office. "Open the door."

Howard looked shocked, "Are you certain, Mr. Doyle?"

"Open the door!" Frank shouted.

The sounds on the outside of the door stopped. As Howard opened it, Lacy saw a bedraggled, unshaven man hunched on the patio. A few years of New York subways had taught Lacy to recognize the wild, crazy look of a truly angry drunk. For a minute she thought perhaps he might be the man that almost body checked her the night she arrived at the inn. She shivered, trying to remember some moves from her kickboxing cardio class, but glancing at over she felt better.

Frank stood in the entrance way, feet at the width of his impressive shoulders, arms folded in front of his chest; he had nothing about him that showed fear. The only emotion she could sense from the steel solidity of his stance was anger, or maybe annoyance. In the distance she saw two guards, dressed in black, standing off to either side, batons at the ready. She could just make out the shapes of two more guards on horseback closing in from the front lawn. She didn't recognize these men and in fact hadn't seen any guards in her time there so far.

"I want you to sit quietly until the police come... They'll have a nice, safe cell for you tonight," Frank said to the man.

The man started to rise, "You can't keep her from me!" he shouted.

Frank took one step towards him, uncrossing his arms. The man stopped cold, shrinking down to a heap on the floor.

"If you don't sit quietly, I will lose my temper, Calvin." His face twisted when he said the name, like it was something of disgust he had to spit from his mouth.

The man looked as if he would rise again and then collapsed in tears. "Frank, you need to give her back. She's mine...she's mine..."

"She is not yours, Cal. She never was. I'm not going to speak of it again."

Lacy saw the flashing lights of the police vehicles pull into the carport area. Men rushed to the door and handcuffed the man, putting him in a cruiser. Then they returned to speak with Howard and Frank.

When he was finished giving a statement, Frank turned to Howard.

"I'm sorry, Mr. Doyle, I don't know how he made it past the gates..."

"Don't worry about it, Howard. Have maintenance take a look at that door in the morning. I want no traces."

"Consider it done. Good night, Mr. Doyle."

Frank walked away, until he saw the Lacy sitting on the steps. "Show's over." he said brusquely.

Lacy's face flushed red; she turned and ran up the stairs.

"Lacy, wait! I'm sorry! I..."

Back in her room, Lacy buried her face in her pillow. *How dare he? I'm his guest! I don't even know who "she" is and still I trusted him, I wanted to be there for him! I'm so stupid!*

After what seemed like forever, Lacy finally calmed herself and sleep overtook her.

Chapter 16: Don't Go

The sunlight was streaming brightly through the lace curtains again the next morning. After darting glances about the corners, verifying that she didn't miss anything, Lacy picked up her bag, straightened her shoulders and marched into the hall. Continuing down the stairs, she laid the key on the counter in the lobby, thankful that she didn't see

Howard just now. She said to the clerk, "Lacy Stockton, checking out. Could you have my car sent around?"

"Oh, Miss Stockton, I have a message for you." the clerk said. He handed her a small envelope.

She took the envelope with a quick "Thanks." Swinging her sunglasses from the top of her head down to cover her eyes, she turned and walked briskly across the polished marble and out the front door. Once she stepped into the sun by the fountain, she opened the envelope and began to read the words on the familiar card stock.

Lacy,
Please don't leave without giving me a chance to explain or at least say goodbye.
Frank

Just then she heard the drum of horse hooves racing across the lawn. Looking up, she saw Frank, on a horse at least three hands taller than Daredevil. Apparently he was an early riser as well. She cursed herself silently for not setting the alarm earlier. He raced towards her, just as her car was pulling around the corner by the valet. When the driver saw Frank canter into the area, he slowed. Easing down as he got to the fountain, Frank jumped from the side of the horse before it was completely stopped, grabbing the reigns and walking towards her.

"Wait! Wait, please. Lacy, please, I'm sorry. I was upset. I know you must be confused..."

"Confused!? Confused Frank? The only thing that confuses me is that you would think for one minute that I would stand being talked to like a mere annoyance! Like some child that snuck out of her room and interrupted the adults' party!" She shook his message at him and pointed it at the horse. "And this little fairytale intervention of yours doesn't make everything ok. Or change the fact that last night I wanted to be there for you and I was scared! I don't know what's going on around here, but I'm leaving. I have enough for the article and I'm sure your clients, whoever they are, will be more than satisfied with everything here, especially if the host is unavailable!" She was almost crying now. It was so hard to control her feelings with him.

He touched her hand gently, taking it in both of his. "Please, Lacy. Please, I don't think you're an annoyance. I was a fool. I guess I was worried about it showing up in print somewhere, or...I don't know. But I will explain everything if you give me the chance and just a little more time. I'm asking you because it's truly important to me to have you here, especially these next few days."

She wiped her eyes quickly, pushing tears away before they rolled down her cheeks. Looking into his eyes, she saw he was speaking truthfully. His face was pink and he was breathing heavily. She caught her breath and looked down at the white gravel. Quietly, she spoke, "Frank, I don't want to cause problems in your life."

"You don't cause problems. Just the opposite! You lift it; you've made these past few days so much more exciting and gratifying. Lacy, please...I'm truly sorry to have frightened and confused you. I will make it right. Please trust me?"

She felt herself weakening. She thought about her own somewhat childish reaction last night; storming upstairs, throwing a tantrum in the bedroom, sneaking off in the morning. She sniffed and then her face broke into a smile. "I'll try..."

He smiled immediately, throwing his arms around her and sweeping her off the ground in a great, whirling hug. She felt the world become buoyant, colorful and fast. They were heaving with laughter as he set her down again, slightly dizzy and blushing.

"Thank you so much." he said, with a big smile. "Listen, it's going to be a very busy few days. I will explain things as much as I can and as soon as I can. In the meantime, try to relax. I still have you down as coming to the ball, right?"

"Yes...yes, you still have me," she said, stopping there and smiling knowingly. She was a fool to think she could stay mad at him. *I wonder how much of my anger was actually my own embarrassment?*

"Great. Robert!" he turned towards the valet. "Could you see that Miss Stockton's bags get put back in her room and that her car gets put safely back in the garage?"

"Of course sir," the young man answered, smiling as well.

"I'll see you for dinner, ok? Eight sharp!" He shook her hand wildly and, grabbing the reigns of the mighty horse standing idly by, he strolled quickly towards the stables.

"Ok!" she shouted back at him, laughing in spite of herself. Turning to the young man, she asked, "Is he always like this?"

"Actually, Ma'am, I've never seen him this happy, or this relaxed..."

They both laughed and Lacy turned back towards the hotel. She could smell blueberry muffins from the entrance way and imagined creamy hollandaise sauce running over eggs Benedict, realizing it was time for breakfast. It seemed that everyone who caught her eye had a smile for her. *This place certainly makes it difficult to leave,* she mused.

Chapter 17: The Town Beckons

After breakfast, Lacy decided it was finally time to tackle the town. Grabbing her bag and checking it for her camera and notebook, she headed downstairs, stopping to ask for her car to be brought around again. When she saw the worried look on the face of the attendant, she made sure to add, "Just a spin around town..."

Driving out of the gates she turned right, heading back towards town. It was a perfect day for exploring; bright golden sunlight with some puffy, white taffy twists passing high in the atmosphere. There was a light, cool breeze and she had the top down again, leaving the windows up. She drove at a leisurely pace, inhaling deeply; feeling more relaxed with each breath. She couldn't say she was stressed exactly, but with everything that had transpired it was wise to get outside, clear her head and try to put things together. She was conscious of her defense mechanisms. *I don't want to jump to conclusions just to satisfy my curiosity. I need to at least give the man a chance to explain...but who was that crazy guy? And who is this woman they are fighting over? I wonder if this town has anyone with loose lips...*

She pulled into a parking spot by a little café, pastries and brightly colored coffee tins displayed in the front window. The town wasn't packed with people, but it certainly wasn't empty. She could understand why it never dropped off too much. Adorable was the best word to describe it.

West Dobley would clearly be a regular stop for anyone living or traveling nearby and a destination for anyone else. It seemed ideal in so many ways; with a number of attractions for families and lovers. Even quiet soul-searchers wanting a few hours of peace would find it a place to feel comforted and whole. It reeked with built up memories, strangely even by those who'd never seen it, as Lacy hadn't. The town was a blend of familiarity and freshness.

Construction was ever present, but in a small scale and handled discreetly. It delivered more eagerness to what was coming than hindrance or nuisance. Lacy knew that any place she walked into would likely be stocked with regulars, as well as people happy to discover it for the first time.

The town center was crammed with smaller inns, boutiques and stores, restaurants and antique shops. It was much larger than it looked. There were wide, manicured main streets and smaller, coveted alleyways, a number of which were blocked off to automobiles via granite blocks and signage. It formed a network of curling cobblestone walkways, thick with shops, benches, fountains, sales carts and flower pots brimming with color. *I might just get lost here and stay forever*, Lacy mused, spinning around slowly next to the car to get her bearings and take in the atmosphere of the area.

She didn't even bother to put the top up, seeing the number of people on the street and picking out horseback-mounted police officers within sight. She knew there were more on foot somewhere and had a very secure feeling wash over her. *Let's start here,* she thought, walking first into the *Hibernatin' Bear* children's bookstore that she had seen from the street on that first night, driving through town.

She was surprised to see that the store's interior was designed to give the impression that visitors had left the cobblestones and were walking into a forest. There was a yellow-gold, faux-brick walkway spinning through green carpeting. It wound around large, tree-shaped columns with bookcases carved into the sides. There was greenery and brown branches hanging overhead and different parts of the ceiling were painted to reflect either a starry night sky or a bright, blue, sunny day, depending on which side of the store you were on. Storybooks perfect for bedtime reading were carefully displayed on the night side, with the day side reserved for more adventure themed tales.

One wall was painted like a sunset and off in another corner stood a tree house, big enough to walk into, stocked with child friendly furniture and couches for reading. There were a few short steps leading to several slides built into the walls of the tree. Children were running around ecstatically or cuddled on their parents' laps listening to a story. In another corner several were seated on steps laid out in a semicircle, like a miniature amphitheater. A woman in a bear costume paced back and forth in front of them, reading a story aloud and adding her own dramatic movements. The children were transfixed. A number of parents waited patiently in a line to buy the book the woman was reading. Lacy caught herself staring around the store in disbelief, when she heard a quiet, feminine voice behind her.

"First time?" the voice asked. "I can always tell when it's someone's first time in our store." Lacy turned to see a kindly woman smiling, her silver hair bobbing on her head as she nodded.

"Yes, yes it is. I've never seen anything like it. It's amazing. I'm Lacy Stockton." Lacy extended her hand and shook the woman's as she added, "I'm here doing a story on the inn, Haven. I'm including some information about the town for background and local color. Sort of *a, what to do while you stay at Haven* type of thing. This is quite a place you have here. I'll definitely be including it."

"Yes, we're very proud of it. Mr. Doyle helped a great deal with the concepts, but he encourages us to make our own creative input. My name's Grace. Feel free to look around, but if you are looking for a more...*grown up* book store, you might try the *Cocke & Crowe*. It's on White Street, more of an alley, really; E's on the end of the words, so just look for a wooden sign; red rooster, gray crow. It's just up the road a bit, on the right."

"Thank you...Grace? Could I ask you something? I hope I'm not imposing, but I was hoping you could tell me a little about...about Mr. Doyle." *Heavens! Am I blushing?*

Grace tilted her head to one side slightly and looked Lacy over head to toe, settled on her eyes and gave a little smile. "Thought you might ask that."

"Am I that transparent?" Lacy asked apologetically.

"It's not your fault, he's quite a man. We'd better sit." Grace took her arm and walked her to the big tree in the back of the store. She sat down on one of the low couches and gestured for Lacy to do the same. Most of the children were crowded into the amphitheater on the other side of the store, with the adults browsing quietly.

"You see dear, he's a good man...truly. That's certain. I sometimes wonder though if he will ever settle down. He comes into town every few weeks and seems to have a different woman with him every time. He keeps his personal life very much to himself and nobody really knows what part the girls play. The odd thing is that the ladies are all so...different. I mean age wise, looks, walk of life. They almost seem random except for the look in their eyes... Glancing about, nervous, that kind of thing... Some folks around town amuse themselves by thinking the women are royalty hiding from the paparazzi, or relatives, or winners of some kind of contest...draw a number from a hat in Boston, wind up with a weekend date with Frank Doyle in New Hampshire, that sort of thing." She laughed, a hearty, high-pitched roll, as she said this last part. "I once asked Mr. Doyle, when he was in town looking things over, where his "girlfriend" from the week before was...he said, "My *friend*, Grace...my *friend* is out of town, but may return someday." I always got the feeling he wanted to tell me more, but, like I said, he keeps his personal life *personal*. So, alas, no fun for old gossips like me." Catching a downward glance on Lacy's face, she said, "Don't you worry, honey. Mr. Doyle's a bit private, but I don't think he's a womanizer. And he's definitely no fool. You just keep that pretty face around; he knows a good thing when he sees it."

Lacy felt her blush returning. "Thank you Grace, that's very kind."

"Not at all." Grace said, standing. "I have to get back to work; we've got a children's poetry workshop in a few minutes. Enjoy your stay, enjoy the town, make sure you get a pastry at *Denise's* and feel free to stop in again."

Lacy stood up, shaking Grace's hand again, "Thank you, I'll do that." The story hour had ended just as she was shaking hands with Grace and as she made her way towards the door she saw children running about as if the books were free candy. She smiled again at Grace, who was simultaneously patting a child on the head and using her free hand to point a couple towards another corner of the store. Grace stopped pointing just long enough to manage a quick wave. Lacy nodded and walked out into the sun.

Chapter 18: Mulling it Over

She strolled around town, taking her time, patiently feeling the space and keeping an eye open for angles or interesting subjects to capture by camera. She struggled to maintain focus, wishing her mind was as easy to operate as the lens, but she kept hearing what Grace said. *Who were these women? And let's face it; the real question here is what am I going to be to him? Am I a pleasant distraction, good for a week of fun and then what...I go back to New York never to return? Have I already let this whole thing get blown out of proportion? Ugghhh. Pull yourself together, Lacy! Barbara didn't send you here to walk around in a daze!*

Remembering her duty to her friend helped to clarify things a bit for her. She looked around with renewed interest, scribbling notes in her jot pad, pausing every now and then for a good shot. She slowed her pace even further, taking notes on almost every corner. *There's enough here for a guidebook! How am I going to boil this down to background filler?*

Turning onto White Street she saw the storefronts were high enough to create shade in the alley. It was another cobblestone walkway, about seven feet wide, too narrow for cars. She stepped into *The Barrel in the Cellar,* a vintage wine store. The store, like all she had seen so far, carried the theme throughout, retail entertainment at its best. There were three steps down from the front door, leading to brown, glossy tiled floors and large archways of brick. Bright yellow lighting shone off walls stocked with wine racks. On the left was a counter and refrigerated cooler section, stocked with imported and domestic cheeses, several of which were displayed on small cutting boards as samples. Tins of caviar and other gourmet groceries were easily within reach. She had a brief image of her and Frank stopping here to buy a bottle of wine and some cheese, then popping in at *The Bread Box* across the street for a fresh loaf. The daydream culminated in the two of them finding a hill overlooking the town, to sit and laugh and talk and kiss. Eventually they would make their way back to the cabin, light a fire in the fireplace and...*Lacy! This is a job! Focus!* She straightened her back, finished her notes, smiled at the shopkeeper and walked out.

Turning to the left, she saw the wooden sign with the rooster and the crow on it. Peering in, she saw large, overstuffed chairs, tiffany-style glass lamps and golden oak bookcases stocked with books, some leather bound. On the side of the store nearest the window, there was a bank of cash registers and a case displaying fine stationery and pens. Further beyond that, a ten-foot counter of the same wood, with coffee and espresso machines, jars of loose-leaf teas and a glass case with pastries in it. A small sign discreetly placed in the front of the case said, *"The Cocke & Crowe is pleased to serve pastries from Denise's, baked daily. Please enjoy."*

Again her mind was flooded with images, this time of cozy, rainy days and taking some time alone. She saw herself cuddling in one of those big chairs with a good book, a sweet treat and some coffee. She exchanged a few words with the young woman behind the counter, asked about some of the items on the small menu and strolled out onto White Street again.

The rest of the afternoon went much the same. Almost every store captured her attention. At *From Humble Beginnings,* she looked at educational toys for Josephine, her faux-niece. She settled on an art kit. After purchasing it she walked out, tucking the kit under her arm long enough to take a snapshot of the store front. The window display; teddy bears wearing black berets and painting on little easels, was drawing the eyes of passing children and their parents alike.

Then it was on to *Denise's*, finally. The pastries were everything she had heard from Grace and more. They shone like jewels in the cases, rare blends of ingredients with perfected esthetics. After a Blueberry-cheesecake scone and coffee, she continued her journey.

There was *The Potting Shed* florist's shop, full of shabby-chic chandeliers and candlesticks, assorted antique furnishings and a cooler overflowing with enormous, healthy blooms. She saw all the classic species she was familiar with and a few she didn't recognize.

The *Three Blind Mice* toy store, with primary colors splashed on the walls, was packed with sturdy, well-made toys of heirloom quality. There were rocking horses, strong enough for her to sit on if she wished and there were metal foot-pedal cars, like she remembered having when she was a kid. *Barbara, we're going to have a field day.*

The *Stitch in Time* craft store offered classes every weekend and some weeknights on every imaginable craft; quilting, toile painting, cross-stitching, pottery, knitting, sketching, painting, woodworking and more.

There were countless restaurants serving every sort of fare, cafés in different regional styles, stores that were extremely browser-friendly and overall the whole town was well lit and clean. The fashion boutiques were charming and filled with several articles that for some reason she felt extremely attached to at first site. She purchased a few things, including a thick weave cashmere sweater and some black slacks that hugged her figure. There were frequent, clean, public restrooms, places to picnic and trees along the sidewalks for shade. There was a little open courtyard in the center of town, with a large gazebo, proudly displaying its promise of free concerts on weekends during the summer months.

Lacy grew more and more amazed as the day went on. She could see things; little details she just knew were the result of Frank's personal touch. She couldn't comprehend being able to manage such a huge number of people and tasks effectively.

The natural flow and care of thought was evident everywhere; in the sweeping lines and styles of the streetlamps, in window displays and benches, in storefronts and open doors. Each piece of the puzzle was placed just right and formed a complete package. *This town is more like a theme park. How does he do it? And the inn too? No wonder he's always busy. I'll be certain to tell him I'm impressed at dinner.* She deposited her packages on the passenger seat. Walking around the car to get in, she realized it had been quite a day and she was happy to be off her feet for a few minutes.

She forced herself to drive calmly back to Haven, knowing she was looking forward to dinner but wanting to keep her emotions in check. She tried to convince herself that it was because she hadn't had anything to eat since breakfast, except that delicious scone, but she knew the truth. She wanted to sit across from Frank, look into his eyes and pretend the week wouldn't ever end. *It would be nice to get some direct answers out of him...tonight he'll find me harder to dodge; I am a reporter, after all...* Besides, she had some new weapons at her disposal now, having spent the day in West Dobley. She felt sufficiently armed with a better sense of who Frank was and what he was capable of.

It was just beginning to get dark as she pulled onto Strawberry Lane and followed the familiar sweep of the driveway. Some high clouds had built up and the fading sun was taking on a cooler color than prior in the week. Lacy was quite fond of the seasons in New England. She recognized the coming of fall, a graceful creep of color over the landscape and a bit of a chill in the night air. She had a brief flash of wearing her new cashmere sweater and Frank's arm, hearing him comment on how great she feels. *Barbara, you have turned me into a clone!*

Handing the car keys to the ever present, ever cheerful attendant, she declined the need for assistance and took the packages from the passenger seat herself. She walked across the quiet lobby and up the stairs, her anticipation growing.

Chapter 19: Left Wanting

Once she freshened up and changed, Lacy headed downstairs to the restaurant. Apparently Sanctuary, unlike the rest of the Inn, was open for business. A few groups were enjoying themselves and the air wafting from the entrance smelled wonderful. As she walked in, the maître d' was waiting to seat her. He led her to a table, explaining that Mr. Doyle had not arrived yet and introducing the waiter, who then asked if there was anything he could get her. *How about a martini?* she thought to herself, but instead asked, "How about a Pinot?" adding, "That'd be great," when the waiter suggested a favorite.

With assurances that she'd have it shortly, the man left her at the table and vanished into the kitchen. Returning quickly with the wine and a small tray of warm breadsticks and dipping oils, he disappeared again. Lacy tried a breadstick and sipped the wine, feeling the warmth flood her system. She gazed out the windows at the gardens and the graying sky, watching the trees bend slightly as the wind picked up. She felt quite cozy. Smiling to herself, she sipped her wine again, being certain to flick her tongue on the rim of the glass as Barbara had taught her, to keep her lipstick where she wanted it.

It wasn't until the waiter returned and asked if she would like an appetizer or another glass of wine that she realized she had been staring out the windows for twenty minutes.

"No, no thank you, but could you tell me if there's been any message left for me?" she asked, a bit shocked that the time had passed so quickly.

"Yes, of course, Miss, let me check." the waiter said hurrying off again.

Looks like I caught you, Mr. Doyle. Perhaps you don't have everything under control as you would have us all believe. She smiled slyly as she weighed teasing him about it later. She was still smiling when the waiter returned and told her, in a hushed voice, that there were no messages waiting for her at this time. She nodded and he walked off.

By a quarter-to-nine, the smile had worn off. Her dates in New York had been awful, that's for sure...*but at least people in the city respect your time enough to let you know when you're wasting it, or theirs, for that matter.* She had to come to grips with it, she was being stood up.

She eased up from the table, feeling somewhat embarrassed and mentioned quietly to the waiter *(couldn't he take a break or something?)* that she was returning to her room and would be putting in an order for room service. The waiter nodded with an assuring statement, remembering her name. He said something about seeing that it was all taken care of, but she was barely listening at that point. She strode quietly out of the restaurant and up the stairs.

Chapter 20: Voices Carry

By the time she rounded the corner at the top landing she was flushed and her heart was pumping adrenaline through her veins. *You're lucky you didn't make it, Frank. Matter of fact, if you were standing here in front of me right now, well I'd...* Her train of thought was interrupted by a scuffling sound to her left. It seemed to be coming from the hall leading to the other side of the inn. Having grown accustomed to having the place to herself, she was somewhat shocked and curious. She slipped her heels off and holding them in her left hand, she crept over to the corner, risking a peek down the hall.

What she saw both confused and troubled her. There was Mr. Francis Doyle, with his arms around a woman. He held her in an extended embrace, then holding her shoulders and looking her face over, he spoke in a hushed tone, after which she nodded and turned away, closing the door. With that he began walking down the hall towards Lacy.

Lacy glanced around and quickly hid herself in a utility closet tucked into the wall on the landing. She held her breath and waited. She heard him pass the closet. She didn't move until she heard the tick of his shoes on the staircase. Only then did she ease the closet door open, glance toward the stairs to check that the coast was clear and walk quietly, but hastily to her room. After locking the door, she marched to the phone and dialed room service. As soon as someone answered she said, "This is Lacy Stockton, I'm staying upstairs in room eight. I would like a large brownie sundae, vanilla ice cream, extra whip cream, two cherries and no nuts please. Thank you."

Hanging up the phone, she turned to the closet and started to hastily pack again, blinking back tears. About halfway through, with clothes leaving a jaunty trail between the closet and the bed, she stopped herself. Remembering her overreaction earlier, she suddenly felt ashamed. *What would Barbara say? She'd say I was being ridiculous. I have to admit it doesn't feel right to be angry, as much as I want to be...perhaps there's another explanation? And a sundae? After that scone at lunch? Oh, I don't care!*

Paused in thought, she barely heard the soft rap at the door and a quiet voice saying, "Room service for Miss Stockton." She tossed the white silk top she had in her hands onto the bed with the others, and then realized it wasn't a top but a negligee. She grabbed the comforter and yanked it over the pile of clothing as best she could. Then she walked over and opened the door, turning away as she did, so the waiter wouldn't see the frazzled look on her face.

"If you could just place it there," she said, motioning to a folding luggage stand next to the writing desk. "Thank you."

"Could I stay for a moment and talk with you?"

Chapter 21: Humble Pie...and Ice Cream

Surprised to hear someone speak, Lacy turned and saw Frank, holding a tray with an impossibly large brownie sundae and a small bottle of champagne on it. She watched him carry it, carefully picking a safe path to the luggage stand through the piles of clothes on the floor. After he placed the tray down, he looked around the room, then at her and said, "You know, we offer laundry services here..."

A tiny laugh briefly burst out, but she caught herself feeling the tears welling up in her eyes. She tried to control her voice, but found words spilling out and rushing together frantically.

"Frank, what's going on? You missed our dinner date and I come upstairs and see you holding that girl and I realize it's your inn and maybe you're accustomed to whisking women away here and filling their head full of seductive notions, but I came here to do a job and you had no right to make that something else unless you were really interested and you never talk and you never tell me anything and...and...and I think I need to leave."

"Lacy..." he began, slowly walking towards her with his arms extended.

Not trusting her resolve when imagining his arms around her, she backed away a step, raising her arms. "No. No touching..." dropping her hands to her sides, she added quietly, "Please don't make this harder on me Frank. I gotta know what's going on."

She managed a quick glance then looked away again. "I'm a *journalist* Frank...but even if I wasn't...I think I...I think I deserve to know what's going on." She looked up at him, hoping she didn't sound desperate.

"Lacy, you're right. I'm sorry. I never meant for you to have to put up with this. I don't have any right to ask it, but please, just give me one more day. The day after tomorrow is the party and I really want you there. No...I *need* you there. You gave me another chance before. If you could trust me a bit further, I'll explain everything. I would tell you now, but...I can't. I know you're scared, but you don't have to be."

"Frank...I don't know what you're afraid of, but if you think I'm *that* kind of journalist, you can rest assured that it's not the case."

"Lacy, if I know one thing for certain, it's that you are definitely not *that kind* of journalist. You've been wonderful. You bring a light to Haven that I've never seen in it. I want nothing more than for you to be fully aware. Listen, you need tomorrow to write the article, right? Take a day, do what you came here for and then enjoy the evening. You deserve it! After the party I will tell you everything."

Lacy watched his eyes the whole time he was speaking. The soft, intelligent glow told her he was telling the truth, but she was fighting years of the wrong dates with the wrong guys. In the end, it wasn't really a decision. Somewhere during the few seconds of silence, while her desire to fall into his arms fought the urge to put up defenses, she found herself locked on his eyes. She gazed at the small wrinkles at the corners and found herself thinking about the last time she saw him smile. *Do we ever really make decisions? Why is it I feel I've known all along what I was going to do...that I was just waiting for the right time to do it?*

"OK, Frank. I came here to write the cover article and I'm not going back to New York without it. But you have to promise to make good, or...or so help me I'll trash this place in the article so bad you'll have to sell it to Holiday Inn."

When Frank heard her he smiled and seeing him smile she sniffled and almost laughed out loud. "We can't have that," Frank said as he stepped slowly towards her. Somehow she felt his hand on hers. She watched, in a daze, as he gently lifted her hands to his lips and kissed them like the other night, but without the joking. "I know, I know...no touching, right? Forgive me."

"Just this once," she replied, barely audible.

"Thank you, Lacy," he said as he backed to the door. "Enjoy the sundae, I hope it hasn't melted. Be sure to call down for another if it has. Good night."

"Good night, Frank." *Is he leaving already? Thank God for sundaes...*

After he left she turned to the room, still in a shambles with clothes piled everywhere. She re-piled her things on the suitcase and grabbed the tray, setting it next to the tub while she drew a bath. Settling into the warm water, she thought back to the dates she walked out on, the guys she never called back, the ice water she threw in the face of one particularly disrespectful man at a horrible dinner. Then her thoughts turned to Frank and she wondered what was different about him. *Oh, everything, that's what.*

She smiled, leaned over the side of the tub to grab a spoon of the thick, rich ice cream and settled back into the billowing foam. She tried to brainstorm on the article, returning occasionally to the image of him kissing her hands before saying goodnight. Finally she gave up on work and went to bed, still confused over the day's events but willing to see if things looked different by the light of day. *It worked this morning...the town was amazing. Let's see if the magic continues.*

Chapter 22: The Write Thing

In the morning, Lacy woke up early, rang for breakfast (blueberry scone, coffee, yogurt, one boiled egg) and took a quick shower. *No time for drama, Stockton. We have a job to do!* While she was toweling off, room service arrived. She had the young man place it next to the desk. After thanking him, she followed to the door, placed the "Do Not Disturb" knob hanger outside and slid the deadbolt into place. She realized that this was more of a psychological barrier than a physical one, since she didn't expect any visitors and the inn had been mostly empty for her entire stay. Turning to look at the laptop on the desk, she narrowed her eyes. The screen seemed to glare back at her, challenging her. It was already powered on, word processor program flashing a small black cursor on a blank, white page.

For a brief moment she remembered what it was like when she was just starting out, fighting distractions, writer's block and her body's limitations. But Barbara had taught her the magic of good habits, rituals and preparation. She knew just what to do. Walking purposefully toward the clothes still piled on the suitcase she began to toss items to the side.

Rummaging about for a minute or two, her fingers felt the familiar touch of a long, green, wool sweater, well worn and complete with matching belt and pills of fabric on the elbows. Dropping the robe, she pulled on a tank top and her pajama bottoms and twisted her hair up into a knot, stabbing it with a pencil. She did trunk twists, arm circles, face stretches, ten jumping jacks, neck circles and a short, furious run in place. Then she pulled on the sweater.

Sitting down, she pushed the laptop to the side and began to spread out notes, brainstormed lists, a few printed photos, some postcards and a colorful tourist map she had grabbed in town. A bite of scone had her mouth occupied while she gazed over the arrangement of media. As an afterthought she stood and walked quickly to the bedside table, picking up her cell phone and switching it off.

Back at the desk, she reached over to open the window above it. The air, cool and crisp, was refreshing and seemed to charge her. She grabbed a notebook and started making an outline, stopping every couple of minutes for a bite of scone, a sip of coffee, or to shuffle through the papers and photos.

After a few productive hours, she paused to stretch her arms above her head and returned to the suitcase. She pulled out tight workout pants, a sports bra and a bright pink t-shirt and proceeded to change. Pulling on running sneakers, she called the restaurant and ordered lunch to be delivered in one hour. After a final glance at the outline, partially committing it to memory, she walked out. She wanted to allow the bones of the article to rest with her a while, during her run.

She ran down the long path, through the gardens to the stables. Lingering there for a few minutes, she chatted with Pierre and gave Daredevil a much-appreciated pat down and a carrot. Then it was off through the gardens and to the inn again at full speed. Fifteen minutes later, catching her breath outside of the restaurant, the smell of the delicacies being prepared in the kitchen caused a quick glance at her watch. *OK...half hour to shower up and revamp the outline*.

Hustling upstairs and showering quickly, she pulled on fresh pajama bottoms, another tank top and the green sweater. She had put her hair in a ponytail for the run, but now it was twisted into the towel turban on her head. Pulling the towel off, she secured her long brunette strands back into the bun, with the pencil once again holding it firmly in place.

She almost didn't hear the knock on the door signaling the arrival of lunch, the server had to knock twice. Shaking herself out of her mental focus long enough to have the food placed next to the desk, she thought of diving back into the project immediately, but a wisp of the scents coming from the tray forced her to taste it.

It wasn't a complicated, fancy meal. *But just right,* she thought, taking a bite of the grilled sandwich, savoring the fresh basil, tomato and feta cheese between the pressed, herbal bread. A sip of the thick, creamy tomato soup followed, which she had requested in a large mug. She spent the next twenty minutes gazing out the window, playing the words out in her head and snacking on her lunch.

Eventually, she pushed the tray towards the side of the desk a bit, shuffled the notes, pictures and outline to the other side and pulled the laptop to center stage. *Now it's time to show Barbara that she didn't make a mistake in sending me here. And show Frank that I'm a professional...at least some of the time.*

The next few hours consisted of rapid typing, short moments of mental brainstorming, brief pacing about the room and the sorting of digital pictures. By six o'clock that evening she had her draft ready and wanted to step away from it for a while. She had purposely not asked Frank to meet her for dinner. If this was to be her last night in the inn, she wanted to savor the pleasures it had to offer as a true guest might. That was the personal touch Barbara wanted reflected in the article. Letting her mind wander resulted in being drawn to the events of the night before; the woman down the hall and the discussion with Frank. However, she managed to pull it back to the job at hand, sometimes even surprising herself with her level of discipline.

Somehow this had become much more than an assignment. Not that the story wasn't a big enough deal. As the annual award issue, it was like being on center stage; very likely to lead to other opportunities if handled correctly. But more than that; being in New Hampshire had been a growth, a rebirth. In under a week, she had taken up riding again, fell in love with an entire town and met somebody, who, regardless of the drama, secretiveness and confusion, was nevertheless somebody very special. So yes, she was focused on the work, but at the same time, hidden behind the discipline driving her hands to flash across the keys, there was a storm of emotions raging. She was simultaneously hopeful, concerned, confused and even grateful.

Happy with the draft, she dressed for dinner and headed down. She felt like celebrating, and ordered a sumptuous, but well-deserved dinner of grilled lobster tail and garden vegetables, with a large glass of delicious German white wine, which the house sommelier had chosen to go with the meal.

Warmed by the wine, the daydreams and a quiet dinner, she took a few minutes to walk in the gardens. She walked slowly, digesting the food and her emotions, allowing things to synchronize and her head to clear. She knew the draft would need some work when she went upstairs and she wanted to be prepared to see it with fresh eyes. Casually strolling to her room, she glanced only once down the wing that was the site of so much havoc the night before. Then it was back to the keyboard, the pajamas and the green sweater, sitting down to read over the document that reflected a week's work.

Chapter 23: Bearing Gifts

Putting the finishing touches on the rewrites left Lacy very pleased with the efforts of the day. She briefly contemplated another sundae, but decided the calories from dinner were more than enough. She was about to settle in when she heard a quiet knock. Her heart raced and she had to stop from sprinting to the door. She opened it, but was surprised to see Howard standing there, holding a large, white box.

"Howard? What's going on?" she asked, hoping he didn't catch the slightest glimmer of disappointment that had flashed across her eyes.

"I'm sorry Lacy," he said. "I know you were probably not expecting anyone, but Mr. Doyle wanted you to have this. He said to let us know if it needs any adjustment in the morning." He handed her the package and said goodnight.

Lacy opened the box and recognized Frank's stationery resting on the folds of tissue paper.

Dearest Lacy,
Something for the ball tomorrow...I hope you like it.
Frank

She set the box on the bed and lifted the tissue stamped "Isaac Mizrahi" in gold script, revealing a cream colored, pearl-beaded dress. She gasped, lifting the dress and holding it in front of her by the full-length mirror. She couldn't resist and decided to try it on right then and there.

The sculpted front was fairly low and it dipped wildly in the back. The luxurious fabric was cut on the bias and tailored to hug her figure, draping perfectly to the ground. She was beside herself as she hung the dress in the closet and lay down in bed. After a few minutes she got back up and stared at the dress again, lightly fingering the beadwork before returning to bed. *Boy does this guy know how to apologize... Barbara is going to need oxygen when she sees this...*she smiled to herself and drifted off to sleep.

Chapter 24: The Rush

Lacy awoke to the beeping sound of a truck backing up somewhere. Glancing out the window she saw bustling gardeners, wheeled carts of equipment and preparations for the coming festivities taking over the estate. *The party! Wow, that was fast...What a week!* Turning from the window to look at the dress hanging in the wardrobe, she felt the excitement growing in the pit of her stomach. *This is going to be quite a night.*

The event was to be completely catered by the restaurant, which was closed for the occasion. The other hotel staff had been given the night off, with the exception of a volunteer skeleton crew, who would receive holiday wages for choosing to work. Judging by what Lacy could pick up, most of the staff that had accepted the break from work had chosen to return to the inn as a guest for the black tie event.

The different trucks in the driveway hinted at the planning for the evening. There were flower arrangements, tables to be set with hot and cold hors d'oeuvres in the halls, an espresso bar with an enormous gleaming copper machine and even a full, fifteen-piece orchestra. No expense had been spared and Lacy understood that everyone from senators to celebrities would be in attendance. The inn and its charismatic owner had many generous and famous patrons and friends.

The rest of the day seemed to rush by in a blur; a trip into town, finding the perfect shoes, bag and accessories to match the dress, coordinating with Barbara. Getting back to the inn before four o'clock had meant running most of the day, but as Lacy settled into the warm bath at a quarter past, she was confident that the pace of the day had been worth it.

She thought back to the day that Barbara had taught her this, another of her "tricks". It was years ago; her first time attending the Governor's Ball. Barbara had insisted they get a hotel near the event, even though it was just on the other side of town. Likewise, she stated that Lacy could do whatever she had to do that day, provided she be at the hotel by four o'clock sharp that evening. When Lacy rushed in the door, packages drooping from her arms and feeling more than a little frazzled, Barbara was waiting with a smile. "Time for your bath."

"What?!" Lacy exclaimed. "I've been rushing around all day and the reason you demanded I be here by four was *to take a bath*?"

"Lacy darling, it's important that you learn this... When you go to a public event, you are representing everything you stand for, as well as our magazine. Most people tense-up, looking stressed and frazzled. I don't care what designer's gown you're wearing or if you have half of Antwerp on your neck, if you aren't relaxed you will come across lacking confidence, character and completely devoid of charm. Now march yourself to your half of the suite, take a nice hot bath for *at least* a half an hour and proceed to get dressed. The ball starts at seven. We'll be arriving at a quarter to eight and not a second earlier." Lacy had retreated to her bathroom laughing. Barbara had proven her genius once again. They had a great time at the ball and Lacy was certain to follow the same ritual for every major event with the same results.

Before she knew it she was styling her hair. She couldn't remember the last time she wore it up, but that gorgeous dress would flatter her neck, shoulders and back in a way that couldn't be ignored. She curled her hair into thick loops on the top of her head, with a few twirling strands hanging down near her temples. Then she sat at the vanity and began applying her makeup. She made sure to go lightly on color, just a smooth bronzer and some touches of a darker brown shadow above the eyes. Pleased with the tones, she slipped into the dress and shoes, grabbed her clutch and tried not to run down the hall. Barbara would be arriving soon and she couldn't wait to see a familiar, predictable face.

Chapter 25: Thank God for Barbara

"Lacy! Don't you look beautiful! Is that the dress?" Lacy's big smile shined and she descended the last few steps in a whir, rushing into the lobby, meeting the open arms of her friend. Barbara had stopped chatting with the concierge in the middle of a sentence and now waved him off with a charming smile. She grabbed Lacy's arm and walked down the hall wide-eyed. "Can you *believe* this place? Even better than I'd heard! It's like getting a room at the Biltmore! Tell me everything. How are you? Is he nice? Is the town as beautiful as it seems? Where's the article? Tell me you have the rough draft done? I missed you! Josephine misses you and says you *have* to take her out next week to celebrate your cover and her birthday. She says you both must go to tea, like you did last spring, remember? Oh, darling, how have you *been*?"

"Whoa! Barbara, I'll tell you everything, but take a breath! Come with me, you've gotta see this place." The comfort of talking with someone she knew and who really knew *her* had her feeling refreshed and relaxed. "It's only six and the party won't start until at least seven," and to Barbara's questioning look and raised eyebrow she added, "...and we won't be going in until quarter to eight...at the earliest." Barbara nodded approvingly and they both laughed.

Lacy pulled her off towards the restaurant, exiting into the gardens beyond. Ordering tea for two on the patio, she finally got to catch her friend and mentor up on the strange happenings of the week, the article, the town, the subterfuge...everything.

At eight-thirty, they rose to walk back to the inn; Barbara's face an unusual mixture of bewilderment and concern. They paused by the restaurant doors and Lacy looked up at her, calmly waiting for the wise and much needed advice to flow from Barbara's lips and soothe her mind. Lacy knew it was coming. Every time she chased her heart down a dead end street, Barbara had been there to point her back to civilization, always with a measured and appropriate response. She had never let her down before and when their eyes met, Barbara straightened her frame ("Posture is about *who* you are," she always said), softened her face and spoke.

"Darling, this may sound strange to you, but sometimes you have to sit back, enjoy the show and trust that you will do the right thing at the right time. I'm not oversimplifying things, although it may sound that way at first, but we just don't know all the elements in the equation. Believe me, if I had enough information to be clear about his intentions, what he's up to and whether or not it's worth spending another second with him, I'd tell you. But we don't have that. And that means, well...that we wait and see."

"Wait...and see? That's your words of wisdom? Wait and see?"

"Not *just* wait and see, darling. It's not a one-way street. We wait and see what he'll do, of course, but we also wait and see what we will do, *always confident* that we will do the *right thing*. Because you *deserve* to be treated fairly. We *know* your intrinsic value, as a person and a potential mate. Lacy, I believe in you with all my heart. No matter what happens you know you can always count on me to be there. We'll get through this...*you'll* get through this...whatever it is and someday soon we'll be sipping Cosmos and laughing about it together."

She's right. I don't know how she does it, but I always feel better after she lays it out. "Thank you, Barbara. I'm so glad you're here."

"Don't mention it darling. Now come on! I chatted up that concierge and he gave me a peek at the guest list. Did you know that half of Hollywood, Wall Street and Washington are coming to this thing? Let's go show Mr. Doyle that we know how to party!"

They embraced quickly, Barbara squeezing her for an extra second before they turned and walked into the inn.

Chapter 26: Beautiful Chaos

The normally quiet, polished lobby was now stuffed with couture gowns, perfectly made up faces, jaw-dropping shoes and crisp tuxedos. At first Lacy was taken aback, but she noticed her friend out of the corner of her eye. Barbara turned and gave her a quick wink, then set her shoulders and stepped into the fray, lightly grasping two champagne flutes from a server's tray and handing one to her. She followed suit and they made their way to the ballroom.

The musicians were lightly playing from the small stage and guests were happily chatting, laughing and snacking on oysters on the half-shell or canapés of caviar and crème fraiche, smoked salmon and dill. It was a whirl of scents and color: gourmet food, colognes, fine perfumes and crisp linens all blending into a bewitching essence of class and excitement.

They laughed, mingled and thoroughly enjoyed themselves for a few minutes when the room suddenly grew quiet before erupting in applause as Frank Doyle entered and began to canvass the crowd. He was dashing. Not a thread out of place, the tuxedo cut like it had been measured that afternoon and his hair parted and combed with a bit of shine to it.

He walked through the guests with ease, grace and confidence. Shaking hands, trademark smile beaming, managing the crowd, he chuckled lightly and openly with people, as if this were just another night at the inn and he was a guest, like them. People were drawn to him. He shone with clarity and humbleness. He was dodging their congratulations with true humility, seeing to everyone's comfort and all the while, scanning the room.

When his eyes met Lacy's he paused mid-stride, made quick apologies to those around him and turned to walk directly towards her. As the crowds' eyes turned towards her, Lacy tried not to blush, even when she heard Barbara's low whisper, "My goodness, he's coming over! *That's* him?"

"I *told* you!" she hushed back. *Please hurry, please hurry, I don't want to faint on the ballroom floor.*

"Lacy...you look...amazing."

"Thank you, Frank. You look wonderful yourself." She was so glad she had been able to find words. He was watching her closely, holding both her hands in his and not speaking. "It's the dress...thank you. It's so beautiful." she added as an afterthought.

"No...it's definitely *not* the dress. But I'm pleased you like it." He turned to Barbara and Lacy saw her eyes widen as he shook her hand. "And you must be Barbara Livingston. I've heard a great deal about you. Thank you for your help in coordinating everything. It's so nice to put a face to the voice. I'm so pleased you could join us here tonight and I can't thank you enough for sending Lacy. Her keen eye and open heart have made this place truly blossom in the past week."

"Well, I sent my best and I can see I chose the right piece for the space... Mr. Doyle, this inn, this town, is extraordinary. You're to be commended." *Always the picture of calm womanhood...How does she do it?*

"Thank you," he glanced down briefly, then added, "Come with me, both of you." Taking their hands, Frank pulled them, stunned, towards the stage and began calling for attention. "Ladies, gentlemen, this is Mrs. Barbara Livingston, chief editor of House To Home magazine...and Miss Lacy Stockton, the wonderful journalist and talented writer that has done such a careful and heartfelt examination of our little inn and town." The crowd applauded and he continued, turning towards them, "I'm so grateful to both of you, for painting Haven and West Dobley, in such a fine light. And for allowing us the opportunity to bring these fine people together for such a good cause. Incidentally, it was Lacy's idea to use this as a fundraiser. I couldn't be more pleased."

Lacy did her best not to blush, but felt the blood rushing to her face anyway. She hoped the makeup would hide most of the color change and managed a smile. Barbara made a gracious remark about how the inn raised the bar for service institutions worldwide and how they were only too happy to announce that Haven would be detailed in the next issue. The whole time Lacy couldn't take her eyes off Frank. As they stepped down from the stage amidst applause, they were greeted by handshakes from the elegantly dressed people.

Her mind was whirling, but she managed to pick out a few pieces of conversations, mostly; *"...how important what you're doing is, you've got to come to the Red Cross ball this year,"* and; *"Give me a call when you get a chance, Frank has my contact information, we'd love to see what you think of our place,"* and; *"I'll be sure to grab the next issue, if its anything like I think it will be, I may have to hire you to consult on my next script. Location detail and descriptive work. I'll make it worth your time."*

She smiled and mumbled thanks, shaking hands along with Barbara, attempting to get back to the lobby and a glass of champagne. Barbara stayed with her, whispering in her ear as they made their way through the crowd, "That was amazing! Do you realize who that was? This story is going to put House to Home on the map in a big way. Frank is a godsend!"

They were kept fairly busy for the bulk of the evening and Lacy was pleased to see her work having such a positive impact for her career and Barbara's. She could tell this week would change her life in more ways than one. But secretly she just wanted to run up and hug Frank, pull him into the library and kiss him full on the lips. They stole glances at each other throughout the night, but couldn't manage to pull away from the others for a private moment. As much fun as it was to laugh and chat with Barbara and the guests, she couldn't wait for the night to move along, hoping for a few private moments with Frank after the inn was quiet.

Suddenly there was a gasp from the crowd and a loud crash as a platter went sailing from a server's hands, shattering thin crystal flutes and spilling champagne across the middle of the lobby. A stunned waiter faced a man standing defiantly among the dark tuxedos, shirt torn near the collar, chest heaving, unshaven and obviously inebriated, with a slightly wild look in his fierce blue eyes.

Chapter 27: Unwelcome Stranger

Lacy was certain now, that he was the man from the other night. "Frank!" he called out. "Frank Doyle! You homewrecker! Where are you?"

He lurched towards a particular woman in the crowd that matched the build of the woman Lacy had spied in the hall the other night. Grabbing her by the arm, he started pulling her towards the front door. The woman paled and let out a yelp, but they hadn't made it two steps before they were stopped.

Frank himself, having cut through the crowd with impossible ease, spun the man by the shoulder and landed a full right cross on his chin, sending him flying backwards, out cold.

Security rushed from the corners and picked up the man, escorting him out the front door, where

Lacy could already see blue lights flashing from the long driveway. Amidst the mumbles, gasps and confused applause from the crowd, Frank helped the woman to her feet and sheltering her in his arm, led her through the lobby to the library. Howard was waiting with the door open. On his way through the crowd, Frank shouted over the din, "I'm so sorry folks, my apologies; that man is ill and in violation of several court orders, but it's all taken care of now. If you'll excuse me for a few minutes...please, fill the glasses, I'll return directly." With that he whispered something to Howard, who nodded and closed the door to the library once they had gone through.

Turning to Barbara, Lacy saw that even she was too shocked by the activity to comment. A moment later, Howard was before them, speaking in hushed tones, "Miss Lacy, if you and Mrs. Livingston would please follow me. Mr. Doyle has requested your presence in the library. We can go through his private office, out of the eyes of the other guests, if you please."

Too stunned to answer, Lacy nodded and she and Barbara followed him down the hall to the first door after the library, stepping through when he opened it.

"Howard...what..."

"I believe Mr. Doyle will explain everything, Miss Lacy."

"But...are you sure this is –"

"Isn't it funny, Miss Lacy, that sometimes people shut out the world, often when they need it most?" Howard smiled slightly, ushering them through the connecting door and closing it quietly behind them.

Chapter 28: Mystery No More

Lacy and Barbara stood in the back corner of the library. The pale woman was sitting in a chair, lightly crying, while Frank stood with his back facing them. He was leaning over a large table; head hung low, hands still clenched in fists, his knuckles pressing on the tabletop. Turning, he began roughly, "Howard, I thought I told you we weren't to be..."

"I'm sorry...I...I can go...Howard said...are you alright?"

"Oh, Lacy, it's you...thank goodness. Sorry, please come in, you're more than welcome. You too, Barbara. I want you to hear this. Have a seat, please."

The women glanced at each other. There were too many questions to ask so silence prevailed. They made their way awkwardly to the chairs, Lacy choosing the same one she had been dozing in when she first met Frank earlier in the week.

He began. "This is Mrs. Jennifer Doyle," to their stunned looks he added, "my sister in law." The confusion didn't lessen. "The man you saw taken away was Calvin Doyle, my brother. You see, Jennifer's been hiding here. There are a number of bungalows on the property, out past where you've been riding Daredevil. We keep them secret. They are part of a nationwide network that helps families escape from...dangerous situations. My father...he was sick. Alcoholic. Abusive. He used to..."

Frank was quiet for a moment, turning away. When he turned back his eyes had grown glossy. "I couldn't tell you. I've been wanting to. You see, I reached a point where I said *enough* and I helped my Mother escape. We started over together. I knew I was either doomed to repeat the abuse or destined to fight it. Calvin...wasn't that lucky. Jennifer did everything she could, but he wouldn't stop." The woman looked up at him and nodded slowly. Frank continued, "My own brother...No matter how much we do, I will always feel a failure because I couldn't help him. No, it's true. And it's also why I created this inn, why we cater to very demanding tastes. Why the grounds are so extensive and so well protected. This is not a problem that thrives only in the lower classes. We're always watching for signs. Besides, the more money we bring in, the more we can do to help. In fact, several of the good people working here and in the town are former cases that we've helped start over. "

"Frank, I...I had no idea...I'm so sorry." Lacy started to piece together Cherice's emotional response to her compliment and the watchful, wise eyes of several shop owners in town. The ever-present police and guards, the high security and detailed planning, it was all beginning to make sense.

"Don't be sorry. You couldn't have known and out of respect for what we're trying to accomplish, I don't tell anyone. But it's more than that. I mean...that's not all I want to tell you. You see, Lacy, I think I'm falling for you." Lacy felt her own eyes glistening now. "I know we haven't had much time together, but the connection we have feels so strong to me. I've never met anyone I want to protect and impress more than you. I almost feel selfish having you here. I want you. I want you to...stay."

After a moment of stunned silence, she answered, "Oh, Frank...I...I don't know what to say. You're wonderful, the inn is wonderful...the whole town is wonderful and everything you're doing is amazing..." Lacy rose and glided towards him, feeling his arms enveloping around her. "I'm so sorry; I've been behaving like a child."

"No," he corrected, "You've been nothing short of professional; a good woman and a good friend. You've given me more trust than I deserved under the situation and I'm only asking for a chance to earn that trust over time."

"But Frank," Lacy said, as a spark of reality jumpstarted a more logical thinking process, "I have a job...a life in New York. My career is important to me and to others."

Lacy glanced at Barbara to see several tears running down her cheeks and billowing out around her wide smile. "Tush," Barbara said, "I thought this might happen. Frank called me this week with a lot of questions about you and I can't see why you can't mostly work remotely. In fact, I sent you here because I suspected you were ready for the next step. I can't hold you back forever, darling. New York is only a short train ride away and as long as you *promise* never to leave Josephine and me out of the picture, we can work something out. I'm serious though, I expect *constant* contact and visitation rights. Besides," she glanced at Frank and her eyes narrowed slightly, "I've already had him thoroughly checked out, and I have to admit...he's clean."

"Barbara! Why do I feel like the last to arrive at my surprise party? You two already have this all worked out? How dare you?" They were laughing openly now.

Frank raised the bet, "Look, I'll throw in Daredevil. He's yours. He'll never let me ride him again anyway."

"Oh, Frank. Can this really ever work? I'm..."

"You're amazing. That's what you are. And I'll *make* it work. That's what I do. Look, what have you got to lose? Isn't it at least worth looking into? You can't hit a homerun if you don't step up to the plate. Give me a few months. I'll pick up the tab for your apartment in the city and we'll finally have more time to talk, ride and get to know each other. I'm not crazy, I know life is more complicated than the fairy tale experience you've had here in the past week. Three months, tops. If I don't make a believer out of you, you're free to leave the castle walls and we part as good friends. If I do, we talk about visitation rights for Barbara."

Head spinning, heart racing, eyes locked on his, Lacy embraced him warmly, reaching up to meet his lips with hers. "Yes. Of course yes. It's crazy...and no one would have guessed it could happen this way, but yes. I wasn't really ready to leave yet anyway..."

Barbara was at her side now, arms wrapping around her and a kiss planted on her forehead. "God help me..." she whispered. Lacy looked up questioningly. "Who will I find to cover the next flower expo?!" They all laughed at this.

"You'll think of something," answered Lacy, and they laughed again.

. . .

Epilogue: Making the Call

Lacy couldn't believe it had been three beautiful months since that crazy night. So much had happened. She took over a corner of the office and worked mostly from the inn, traveling to the city when necessary. There were video conferences with Barbara, calls and assignments from Hollywood players, entrepreneurs and some of the best periodicals in the country and, all the while spending as much time with Frank as possible...it had all been like a dream.

Now she sat in the hotel's restaurant, looking over some notes for an article she was planning for the *New Yorker* and sipping dark roast coffee. Frank would be coming back from a meeting in a few minutes and they were going to call Barbara together.

At first she had been afraid that every day would be like a holiday. As much as she felt for Frank, she knew that kind of lifestyle would not be helpful in determining what being together would really be like. But those fears were put to rest.

With her career now booming and Frank's involvement in his many enterprises, they had plenty to keep them busy and space when they needed it. She also saw how eager they had been to find time together and make the most of it.

Her time at Haven was crammed full of special moments, deep sharing and romantic gestures. Pledges weren't necessary to know they would continue working hard to keep each other interested. Nonetheless, she was slightly nervous about making the call. But like Frank had said the night before, "When you know, you know."

Glancing up, she saw him walking purposefully through the restaurant towards her table in his long, smooth strides, that wide, characteristic smile on his face. She couldn't imagine a time when watching him move towards her would be boring.

"Ready darling?" he said, borrowing Barbara's favorite pet name for her. He leaned over to give her a quick kiss before taking a chair alongside hers.

"Ready as I'll ever be." She smiled and he knew she was more nervous about Barbara's reaction than what she was feeling. "She's like a mother to me, Frank," she had said last night. "We'll call her together," he had answered. She was reminded of that feeling he gave her so often; that there was nothing she couldn't tackle without him at her side. She hoped she gave him that same rush of confidence and determination. He told her she did, but she had her doubts, simply because he had grown so important to her.

Lacy glanced out the windows at the rear of the restaurant. Gray clouds were forming, heavy with the first snowfall of the season. Soon the grounds would be coated with soft white cotton and the inn was already being decorated for the holidays. It was going to be a beautiful time to be together.

She sighed, and said with determination, "Ok...let's do it." She dialed, switching to speakerphone and waited nervously for Barbara to answer the phone.

"Lacy? Hello darling! I was just thinking about you. How are you? How's Frank? You wouldn't believe everything going on here, it's been nuts! Are you coming to visit this weekend as planned? I miss you!"

Lacy laughed. "I miss you too, Barbara. I'm still coming this weekend, but I wanted to call you first to tell you something."

"What? What is it? Are you ok? Is Frank ok?" she rattled off questions, concern in her voice.

"I'm fine. And Frank's wonderful. It's just that...Barbara?"

"What is it darling?"

"Well...We have to plan a wedding."

Lacy laughed as Barbara's screams of joy filled the air. She felt tears of joy falling as her friend's torrent of questions began. She looked at Frank, who was smiling as wide as could be and holding her hand. Between trying to answer Barbara's questions and holding on to her emotions, she reflected on the wild story that brought them together and what two people in love can accomplish. It was all too crazy.

Lacy exhaled, her own smile matching Frank's. She had done it. She had launched her career, met someone amazing and is making it work. Squeezing Frank's hand and listening to her friend's heartfelt congratulations, she started to come to grips with this new reality.

OK. Now I know I'm not dreaming. We're in love, he asked, I said yes, and I told Barbara. Now it's real.

The Beginning

Haven's Pasta Carbonara

A hearty Italian classic that helped Frank win Lacy's heart. I hope it does the same for you. Works great with Tagliatelle, but spaghetti will do in a pinch. Serves 4-6.

8-10 oz Pancetta or bacon, diced
1 teaspoon chili pepper flakes
1 and ½ lbs. Tagliatelle (dried)
8 tablespoons grated Pecorino Romano cheese
6 egg yolks
Salt & freshly ground pepper to taste
Freshly grated parmesan cheese to taste
Italian seasoning to taste
Optional: fresh basil, cut into thin strips

1. In a large skillet, over medium-low heat, combine and cook the pancetta (or bacon) and chili flakes until brown.
2. Cook the tagliatelle in a large pot of salted, boiling water, until al dente. Drain, reserving ½ cup of the water used to cook the pasta.
3. Mix the Pecorino Romano cheese into the reserved cooking liquid. Wisk in the egg yolks with a fork, adding salt and pepper.
4. Add the cooked pasta to the skillet with the cooked pancetta, tossing to coat. Add the egg mixture as well, tossing well. Sprinkle with grated parmesan, Italian seasoning and fresh basil, if used, and serve.

Author's Note

I truly hope you enjoyed reading Unlikely
Paradise as much as I enjoyed writing it.
Although this is a work of fiction, I received a
great deal of inspiration for the characters and
story from good friends, some of whom are
beautiful, amazing, talented, loving and brave
survivors/witnesses of domestic violence.

According to the Harris Poll (2006),
approximately 15% (33 Million) of U.S. adults
admit to being a victim of domestic violence.
This can happen to people of any race, age, sexual
orientation, religion or gender and signs of abuse
may be difficult to recognize. The more
informed, observant and active we are, the more
we can help. Together we can end this blight on
our humanity.

If you, or someone you know, needs help in order
to live a life free of domestic violence, please refer
them to:

The National Domestic Violence Hotline
1.800. 799. SAFE (7233)
1.800. 787. 3224 (TTY)
www.thehotline.org

Made in the USA
Charleston, SC
13 July 2012